The Ring of Betrayal

Elle Klass

The Ring of Betrayal

Copyright©2024 by Elle Klass
Published by Books by Elle, Inc.
ISBN: 978-1-951017-43-9
All rights reserved
Editor Dawn Lewis
Cover art Getcovers.com

Author's Disclaimer

Realm Walker

Books in the Realm Walker Series
In the Shadows
The Land of Lost Souls
Hidden Passages
The Ring of Betrayal

Realm Walker Prequel
Heart of Darkness
Soul of Malice

Other Realm Walker Companion Books
The Origin: Marya's Journal
Soul Fire

Realm Walker World Books – coming soon!
Love at Frost Bite
Accidental Ghost: Soul Catcher Vol.1

Other Young Adults Series
The Bloodseekers
Zombie Girl
Hidden Journals
Baby Girl

REALM WALKER

PROLOGUE

Even though Terra had saved the realms there were those who weren't happy…

The night of what became called The Expelling, when Terra and Hank cast the Warlocks, werewolves, and Lols vampires out and sealed the veil between the realms, there were those who plotted against her. They called themselves the Council of Divination.

Shadows swarmed from the corners, whispers breathed through the air, and the black forms oozed to the center of a dark room.

The Ring of Betrayal

A black form in the shape of a giant dragon seethed, "Realm walkers are an abomination. She saved the worthless life forms and she will ruin us." His voice carrying through the spirits in the room.

"How do you propose we get rid of her? We can't kill her or the warlock," another said, its whispers lingering in the air. Death wasn't a bad idea, but it wasn't yet time. They hadn't yet convinced the other. For all his flaws, his hunger for power hadn't yet peaked, as if he had a weakness for the girl.

A short, squat shadow swam to the middle. Its plumage sweeping against the other shadows. They certainly couldn't kill her outright. It would take all their strength and even then, with the warlock on her side, it might not be enough. Trolls usually didn't bother with barbaric responses. They used their brains even in death. "We find the sacrifices used to create realm walkers and reverse the spell." His plumage arched beside his smoky cheek.

Ears with small points designated the fae as she joined the conversation. She found nonfae incredibly annoying. Death didn't change that as they'd suggested something foolish and preposterous. "Suggestions on how we do that. The grimoire is gone and the sacrifices were used in the spell."

The shadows swarmed around the fae, tightening around her. A large shadow rose up above the others. its dark form swallowing them. "Are the fae that incompetent they can't find a grimoire?!" Placing his blame on others.

The fae arched her shoulders back and pushed out her chest. She wouldn't be intimidated by a dragon. As an unharvested soul like the others, her power was equal to his. "Her cave is deep in the lavender seas and empty." Feeling the need to remind the others they weren't the first to think of reversing the spell: "Eighteen years ago the realm leaders searched for the grimoire. It wasn't found then and *he* won't find it now."

"Of course not! It would end him for good. This talk is foolish," responded a shadow, its pointy ears wiggled on the side of its head as they did before it was a lost soul.

"We don't need the grimoire or the sacrifices. We need the stones so we can send the vile one to Marsidia. Forget the girl!" A blob, hiding in the corner, moved towards the swarming group. Its voice calm and collected.

The girl was a nuisance before she knew what she was. Now that she was beginning to understand the breadth of her power she was dangerous, but lacked any desire to reach the full scope of her potential. The vile one they loathed more and could use him to bring down the realms.

The unharvested souls slipped through the walls. A heavy fog covered the stars and light of the moon as they vanished into the night.

REALM WALKER

1

3 months later…

Terra trapped the plasma beam extending from Hank's hands and amplified it, transmitting it into the sky. It spiraled through the clouds until it reached the veil. Lavender light cascaded down the edges of the veil, the rest bounced back. She caught it in one hand and pushed it back to him. It fizzled and vanished as his body absorbed it.

She ripped the seams of the realm open and slipped into the inbetween, emerging behind him. He spun as the realm opened and caught her hands in his. Blue energy grew around him. Terra absorbed it, feeling the warm plasma encapsulate them. Together they forced it outward. The blast pushing the trees backwards, the sound of branches snapping echoed across the highlands.

She could play with magic all day, her command growing with each practice. They'd taken to training in remote areas. The highest peak of Sier within the toppled palace was one of her favorites. The crisp, freezing air whistled in her ears and excited the warm energy between them.

Hank spun Terra around, his braids whipping through the air. She leaned back to avoid being hit with them. He pushed a plasma blade against her throat as she leaned. She smiled and pushed her hands around the flat sides, forcing it away from her as she squared her shoulders. She folded it into a ring and forced it into the snow.

A blue glow snaked around their legs, pulling them together. He let out a scream so high-pitched her ears barely registered it. She gathered the sound waves and forced them into the ground. The earth shook beneath their feet and the force of the rumble cracked the base of the fallen castle, running along the side until what was left of the one remaining upright tower crumbled to the ground.

She enveloped them in a protective shield as he lost his balance and fell onto her.

His hands pressed against the bottom of the shield as their eyes locked.

His firm, muscled legs rested against hers and his face was elevated a few inches above her forehead. His warm breath melted against her and she felt the gentle movement of his chest rise and fall as he breathed. The attraction between them growing since the moment their lips first met months ago.

Terra lifted her chest and sat up on her elbows. Inches between their mouths. In the clear blue, cloudless sky a dragon soared over them. Its wingspan alone was magnificent. Its outline soft and fuzzy from the fog working its way around the inside of the shield. "I think that's enough for today." She dropped it and felt her body fall against the firm, icy earth.

His eyes moved from hers to her chest before he pushed off the ground and offered her a hand.

She wanted to grab his shirt, not his hand, and pull him closer, but fought the urge. He was her guardian, but it was more. Her power was mighty, but with his strength hers was doubled. M'ra's words about a greater danger before dropping into a pile of ash festered in Terra's head. Whatever was happening between her and Hank was important, yet she hadn't completely given in to him. As much as she wanted to, a part of her warned against it.

The Ring of Betrayal

This nagging festered inside her. There was always a catch. Things weren't as they seemed. She hadn't returned to Lols since she sealed the veils and spent most days after classes training with Hank. They still needed the exit Stones of Hovrath and would have to return to Lols to find them. The enter stones were stolen from under their noses by the lottery winning, millionaire, baker, fae/warlock hybrid, Terina.

They managed to get them back and Terra kept them hidden in a world she'd molded in the inbetween. A place only she could get to, unless she brought invited guests.

She dropped the protective shield around Clyde. It's how she kept him safe when they practiced. Clyde scampered between them and stretched his long body along her leg. She reached down to grab him and he scampered away, poking his head into her backpack. A big hint he was ready to go home.

"They might notice this," Hank said, arms folded across his chest as he eyed the fallen tower.

She twisted her mouth. She could fix this. With her hands, she commanded the rubble to slide back into place. Piece by piece lifted from the ground and climbed. What was left of the framing dropped into its slot.

Realm Walker

Hank placed his hands on her shoulders to feed her more energy. His touch sent a wave of yearning and distracted her for a moment. A rock slid down before she caught it and sent it climbing again. This was getting ridiculous. She wanted him, but it wasn't right. Not yet. The stones climbed and dropped faster. They didn't stop until the entire palace was restored. Magic was foreplay and eased the desires burning inside her.

They returned to Provence Academy before the fake sun lowered, in time for dinner. It was great to see all her friends, both purebloods and hybrids, laughing as they sat around the two tables they'd pulled together. In Lols, she'd collected five hybrids for the tribunal. That was her mission. They were to become new members, bringing the diplomat total to forty.

For the past few months they'd been learning about the history of the tribunal and the breadth of their jobs. They'd also been learning to command magic, something they'd started on their own in Lols, but at Provence Academy, with trained instructors, they'd reached new peaks.

Mario had learned control over his shifting. Meesha's guidance had probably been more responsible than what he learned at the academy. Meesha was a pureblood lycan. Strong, powerful, trustworthy, and a great friend.

The Ring of Betrayal

Alex had come a long way. He had more command over his visions, but he insisted some things he wasn't meant to see until the time was right. He'd also warned Terra when they met that powerful people were after her. She couldn't help the chills that spiked her arms when she put his words and M'ra's together.

Warlita, who'd already mastered enchanting magical objects such as stones and precious metals, also had a unique ability to remold metal and rocks as if they were pottery clay.

Dena's ability to speak with insects extended beyond insects. She could communicate with some animals too and was learning to control the power of suggestion. It was a skill she was developing, but mostly it happened when she least expected. Terra thought it worked much like the vampires' ability to mind bend.

Kenya was quickly becoming a master of curses, sigils, and making things move with her mind.

Some of their magic wasn't allowed in Provence but, as hybrids, they had easy access to the realms they were a part of, which Terra took upon herself to help them find out.

It was a field trip when the five were first allowed to stay. They went from realm to realm. Terra figured it would help them define and fine tune their command of magic. The bonus was that they often went to the other realms to practice level 3 magic. What surprised Terra the most was how they were able to enter each realm, like Hank, which she didn't have an explanation for either. In the end it didn't matter. What mattered was connecting with their magic so they one day could be good Lols diplomats because they understood their strengths and weaknesses.

2

Dr. Carina leaned against her desk, one long leg over the other. Her dark hair braided and piled on top of her head, a few loose curls fell across the sides of her face. "The Great War was a time of distrust and pain among the realms. As healers, the elves worked overtime creating new serums and salves to heal those in every realm. It was a time of great discovery, as well as overwhelming sadness."

Terra's mind ventured in another direction, as she already knew of the Great War and why her kind were created. The lecture wasn't about realm walkers, it was about Elfin history. The great healers.

Realm Walker

A tug on her arm brought her mind to Clyde, who was wearing his harness. It helped keep him out of trouble in the class. The leash looped around her wrist. She glanced down but didn't see him. *Clyde,* she called in her mind. Another pull on her arm almost sent her falling out of her chair. She braced her hands on the table and spotted Clyde. His head and front paws were buried in another student's backpack.

She pulled her arm, catching his attention. He glanced at her with his bandit eyes and chocolate ears then leapt out of the backpack, something in his mouth. She gave him the look and he curled beneath her seat.

It wasn't the first time he was curious in class, after all he was a ferret, it was in his nature. Occasionally he took Halsey's sparkly hair pieces and hid them under her bed. The spiteful glare on Halsey's flawless face was worth not scolding him for it. She leaned her arm down for whatever was in his mouth. He dropped it on the floor and it clinked like a ring dropping onto tile, and he chittered lightly at her. She sat up as Dr. Carina glanced her way.

Terra pulled her feet in front of Clyde so no one would see whatever he dropped on the floor. It barely made a sound. Elves didn't have as exceptional hearing as wolves, dragons, and lycans, so she doubted anyone but her heard it.

The Ring of Betrayal

When class ended, she gathered her books and notepad. Dr. Carina's heels clicked on the floor as she drew closer to Terra. "I like Clyde as much as the next person, but if he can't behave himself he needs to stay in your dorm during class," she said with a warning tone.

"I'm sorry. His fur tickled my leg is all. It won't happen again," Terra explained, curious as to what he'd found and dropped on the floor.

Dr. Carina nodded then turned on her heel and strolled to her desk. Terra used that moment to collect what Clyde had taken. Between his paws was something that looked like a feather pen, but the feather was made of metal. He nipped at her as she tried to take it.

She held in a squeak and shook her hand. The surface of her skin wasn't broken, but there was a small pink spot from his teeth. He'd never nipped at her before. She collected her backpack and let him carry whatever treasure it was he'd found.

As she stepped into the hall, Deena, who was also in the class, was waiting for her. "What was that about?"

"The pitfalls of having a ferret."

Deena's eyes dropped to Clyde. "What's that thing he's carrying?"

"His new treasure."

The courtyard and cafeteria were full. She handed Meesha the handle to Clyde's harness and warned, "Don't try and take the thing in his mouth." She always had to leave him outside the cafeteria since the dragon lady cafeteria manager scuffle.

Alex and Warlita were at the kiosk. Since their arrival the school had expanded the kiosk, and added a toaster oven - which meant crispy fries - and a larger refrigerator and freezer. She grabbed a turkey sandwich and a raspberry yogurt.

A smile played on her lips as she watched Halsey, her fae Diama or princess of Navarin roommate, and Bjorn. Terra held herself responsible for the match up. It was the book she found in Navarin that led them on a scavenger hunt to find the realm grimoire and a bit more. They'd been stuck like superglue since.

Halsey puckered her lips in a pouty face as he stole some kind of food from her plate. As far as Terra could tell it was a playful love/hate relationship and would probably end when the school year was over. Halsey would return to Navarin and learn to be a ruler, as one day she'd be queen, and Bjorn? Who knew. He'd probably return to Navarin as well. His mom was a scientist, but she didn't think that put him high enough on the peerage scale for them to continue dating, at least not publicly.

"Mlaka flae," Kenya said as she strolled to the table and took her seat. Since

Terra's friend group grew by five, the entire group grew by five.

Kayln giggled. "Be careful what you say out loud in old fae."

Deena glanced at the two, with an eyebrow raised as if to ask *What did she say?*

Kayln blew it off as she lifted a sandwich-type fae food to her mouth. "What's that thing in Clyde's mouth?"

Terra expelled a frustrated gust of air before explaining. "I don't know. He pulled it out of someone's backpack and won't let me touch it."

"That's not like Clyde," Caspen offered as he sat down, placing his tray with some type of elfin wrap on it on the table. His large, curly afro bouncing as he sat.

Terra shrugged. She had no answer. He was a ferret. It was weird, but she was sure he'd drop it when he got bored with it.

After lunch, Alex grabbed Terra's arm before she stood. "You need to get that away from Clyde. It's enchanted." He had unique abilities and one of them was the ability to see words, even though he was blind, as well as future events with a bit of DNA.

This put Terra on alert. "What is it saying? Is he under a spell of some kind?"

Always quiet and mostly solemn, his face tightened more than usual. "I don't understand the language."

Realm Walker

There was only one place Terra could think of and only one person in Provence she knew to ask. Professor Gwond, her quirky troll magic instructor. He was a walking encyclopedia, brimming over with knowledge of magic. Since the expelling he'd been teaching her level 3 magic. They'd meet in Verboten. She'd learned to transform, as he called it, into other creatures which she'd had some practice with during the invasion. She hadn't brought up the Stones of Hovrath. No real reason, or maybe there was. After the invasion, losing M'ra, M'ra's warning, and the undefined thing between her and Hank, she'd been more reserved.

She returned to her room after lunch and caught up on her homework while she waited for Gwond's office hours. Waiting for Clyde to put down the feather pen, but every time she glanced his way he picked it up and went somewhere else in the room. His behavior was distressing.

She felt like a worried mother by the time she entered Gwond's office. He lifted his head slightly, his round eyes peered at her from behind his glasses. He seemed to read the distress in her expression. "Ms. O'Malley. Is there a problem?"

She blurted it out, as her concern for Clyde was overwhelming. "It's Clyde." Gwond raised his torso and glanced over his desk. "That pen thing in his mouth. He found it in class and won't let go of it. Alex says it's talking to him. When I tried to get it from him, he nipped at me."

With a finger over his mouth, Gwond stood and walked around his desk. The plumage on his tail reached over and stroked Clyde and he chanted something. Clyde growled with the pen in his mouth. A full-on growl. She'd never heard him do that. He was a ferret, not a dog.

"I see." He looked at the clock. "Follow me." His blue sneakers squeaked with each step on the shiny floor.

They walked down the hall and to the first floor, reaching the room under the stairs. The septagonal room with a flag representing each of the seven realms. He peered right, then left. "You are a realm walker." His plumage pointed toward the ceiling. "As a realm walker, there are things you should know and only you can do what I'm going to ask you to do."

She narrowed her eyes. Gwond didn't always follow the rules. It was what she liked best about him.

"Press your hand under each flag."

She did and, after doing so, the floor beneath them dropped, catching her stomach. "What is this? What was that?"

He stepped off the platform. "The antiquity room."

Realm Walker

Light from sconces illuminated various objects on the walls and on tables. The floor-elevator rose back into place so quietly someone could only hear it if they were close by. "What are all these?" she asked in awe.

He pointed towards swords hanging from the wall in leather sheaths. "These were used in the Great War. Some are covered in wolf blood. They were used to kill vampires. Those arrows," he pointed at a few quivers on a table, "soaked in vampire blood."

"What about this?" Terra pointed at an object that looked oddly familiar. It was shaped like a gear for a pocket watch, only it was missing something, oval, and about the size of a rock.

"Part of an ascendant, probably used to travel to Lols." He paused for a moment then continued. "Most of history has been lost and lives in what is left of these artifacts. As a realm walker, you need to understand what life was like before realm walkers, but first we need to free your ferret."

Ascendant – that wasn't a new word. She had seen something about one… Her mind cycled, but was more focused on her ferret. Gwond picked up a small, square, wooden box with a key in the lock from one of the tables and placed it on the ground. Clyde scooted backwards, the feather pen tight in his mouth. His tiny eyes fixed on the box as Gwond pulled out the key and pushed the lid back then walked a couple steps backwards.

Clyde moved closer to the box and paused, glancing at Gwond before he scurried forward and peeked his head inside it. His mischievous ferret instincts couldn't ignore trouble and curiosity which generally went together. Gwond chanted something and the lid dropped closed. It startled Clyde and his jaw slacked and the object fell inside. He barely managed to get his tiny, furry head out in time for the top to come all the way down. Gwond stuck the key back in the lock and twisted, then placed the box back where it came from.

Reading Terra's expression he explained: "The box attracts magic and traps it." She nodded.

Pressing a finger to his cheek. "Where was I?" His eyes twice their normal size through the thick glasses rolled upwards. "Yes, yes. Before realm walkers, all the artifacts had a place and a purpose. People didn't have the same connection to magic as we do now. In order to use it, these tools came in handy. Realm walkers amplify magic. They weren't only created to form and seal the veils."

He went on, explaining how realm walkers were created to be diplomats and they fit that mold well. If lycans needed Aradian wood to build something, the Canidan realm walker would make a deal with the Aradian realm walker. For generations, most realm walkers didn't understand their strength. That matched M'ra's words and it was the great, powerful and, in her opinion, unbalanced Cyrus that helped them realize their potential. Gwond continued explaining how they didn't understand that they were part of the source and amplified it. They fell in line and did as they were told.

It was news to Terra. There'd been clues, but none she caught on to. Possibly it was down to the wild adventure and lack of sleep that many things were fuzzy. Maybe she'd heard them before, but couldn't readily recall.

Lols was alive with magic and M'ra warned her that she was part of the source. There was also the entire spell that formed realm walkers. It all pointed at realm walkers having a unique and strong connection to magic because they were the amplifications of the source. To her, it was overwhelming to think about.

Their existence had been erased and the artifacts stored below the school after the cleansing. They weren't allowed to ever speak of it. He painted a picture of Cyrus, the great realm walker who understood their connection to magic. How they were more than good little diplomats whose existence kept the veils strong. He understood they could manipulate the veils as they pleased, resize the realms if they pleased. There was no limit to what they could do. This scared the purebloods, as they weren't as powerful and dominant as they wished. Their weaknesses and flaws sticking out like a bruised thumb. Realm walkers, as Gwond painted them, were superior in every way.

"People fear those they can't control," Gwond continued his monologue. Cyrus wanted a home for realm walkers, a place they could call theirs. He claimed they were slaves to the realms and should have free will to come and go as they pleased, not when they were ordered. Leaders of all the realms needed them. There was a small group of agitators that whispered in the ears of the leaders, played on their fears that somehow the realm walkers would take over and kill them to keep their realms for themselves. Momentum grew as leaders turned their backs on the realm walkers. They were imprisoned, but bars couldn't hold them so they murdered them all and called it the cleansing.

After, they took every book that mentioned realm walkers, and all enchanted objects, and destroyed them, except the few that had been salvaged by realm walkers before the cleansing, and stored in the antiquity room.

Realm Walker

It seemed they salvaged a lot as she studied the books, scrolls, and objects. "I thought the school didn't exist until after the realm walkers were…" She couldn't say the word. Her mother was one of them.

He smiled. "You've been paying attention. Correct. The school didn't exist."

"Then how? I don't understand."

A thoughtful expression formed on his face. He seemed eager to tell her more. "I will explain that one day. Now is not the time. All you need to understand is that history is important to preserve. You are the only person who can come down here. You may share it with the warlock. Some of these artifacts might be from his ancestors, but you mustn't show or tell anyone else."

She really hated how everyone referred to Hank as 'the warlock'. It was the equivalent of calling her 'the realm walker' instead of Terra. He had a name. She narrowed her eyes and corrected Gwond. "Hank."

As she spoke, her eyes studied the objects in the room. One in particular caught her eye. It was a pickaxe with a pearl handle. The axe head made of wood. "What's that for?" she asked, pointing to the pickaxe.

"Something dangerous. It's a reverser and pulls a soul from its harvested sphere," Gwond responded. His words lacked the caution she expected.

3

erra was perplexed that such a place existed and angry that the realm walkers were destroyed - including her mother, whom she'd never met. After giving birth to Terra she went back to Aradia. It was the only way she could protect Terra. The only others that knew she was pregnant were Rosette, the father who raised Terra, and Cyrus – her biological, realm walker, father.

The father who'd raised her. That was her father, her dad, the man she loved with all her heart. She hadn't known he wasn't her biological father until recently, when M'ra explained it to her before her death. If Terra had been discovered and destroyed the realms would have fallen. Now that she understood more about what she was, she understood how magic existed in Lols. It was her. According to everything she'd learned, Lols hadn't much magic. She thought it was another lie until she understood that she amplified the source of magic. Therefore, was an extension of it.

Hank had the ability to see her magic as a trail and an identifier. Luckily, no one else had that ability.

Destroying that connection to magic is what Merla meant. After the creation of the realm walkers, she warned them that no harm could come to the realm walkers or their descendants. If it did, the realms would collapse. Terra was the reason the realms still existed. A lot was making more sense to her now that she understood what she was. Somehow, the warlocks were central to magic as guardians of the source which was probably at least part of the connection between her and Hank. How they tied in with realm walkers she wasn't 100% sure, but knew the spell that Merla used to create realm walkers was the same spell used to create the Stones of Hovrath and most likely used against the warlocks when the fae locked them in Lols.

Clyde was acting like himself as he ran out of the doors to the school and scampered down the steps. Often times, Gwond deflected things when he didn't think she was ready and other times he pointed her in the direction of other things. She'd learned it wasn't as much about what he showed or told her, but what he didn't. He was an excellent gas-lighter, but she was catching on.

Ready or not, it didn't matter. She was *the* realm walker. Gwond and Hank were the only people she could confide in that had some understanding of what it meant and the huge responsibility it was. Right now, she was a hero, but how long would that last? She felt like she was always looking over her shoulder, waiting for them to decide to cleanse her too. That's why her practice with Hank and Gwond was so important. When and if the time came, she would defend herself. She wasn't going to be used and discarded as her ancestors were. It was a new age for realm walkers, or the realm walker, as she wasn't plural.

Terra strolled to her dorm, allowing Clyde plenty of running and jumping so he'd chill when they got back, her mind a fluster of thoughts.

The secret was out. Everyone knew she was a realm walker. The vampires had positioned themselves to defend her after she saved their realm and gave blood to those bitten by wolves, saving their lives. Their protection wasn't needed. The leaders of every realm bowed to her and showered her with gifts. She felt silly as heck and didn't trust their kindness. It was a double-edged sword.

Terra reached her dorm. Halsey, her roommate, admired herself in the large mirror above her vanity. She hadn't treated Terra any differently and their mostly love but sometimes hate relationship continued normal as ever.

"You look ridiculous with that two-tone mop on your head," Halsey snarled as she pulled a brush through her silky blonde hair.

Her words were true. Terra's hair had grown out so much over the months that it was ready to be trimmed without a buzz or bowl cut to get the dark brown off. Terra couldn't let Halsey get away with the comment, true or not. "Not as ridiculous as you in that pink dress. You look like a fuzz puff," she remarked. The dress, made of a soft, shimmery fabric, reminded her of shag carpet.

Halsey rolled her blue eyes. "There's an elf at Sizzle Cuts in Provence Square who is expecting you after class tomorrow."

"An elf?" Terra chuckled. "Isn't that sacrilegious for them?" It was known elves didn't cut their hair as it was legend that it helped them communicate with plants.

Halsey put the hand mirror down and turned to Terra. "She doesn't cut her own hair. Now, don't miss that appointment. I set it up for you."

The Ring of Betrayal

Terra understood the gist. As the Diama, or princess, of the fae realm, Navarin, that was her gift. Four months since she'd saved the realms, but nonetheless better late than never, and she did need to get the dark hair trimmed away. Rosette had forced her to dye it when she first came to Provence so she could pretend to be an elf. "I'll be there," she promised, easing Halsey's suspicious eye.

Clyde bounced down the steps of the academy. The myrrh-eucalyptus scent blasting Terra's nostrils. The always present odor was a repellent to her. After several months of it, she couldn't take it anymore. She desired the fresh, clean aroma of the ocean. The thought left her brain as a command and almost instantly changed. Sucking in deeply, she relaxed and forced the scent into a bubble around her.

Clyde ran in circles, chasing something in the air. She was happy to see him being himself. A voice interrupted her thoughts. Terra turned to see Hyacinth standing beside her. Terra's vampire friend. They'd become close, especially during the time Terra spent in Drakonia, giving the bitten vampires her blood.

Hyacinth's straight, dark hair lay over her shoulders, a white crop sweater over her chest with a red tank underneath. Her black skirt bounced against her legs as she walked. "Clyde's all better," she remarked as Clyde ran towards Terra then skittered next to Hyacinth.

"Much better. That object was spelled."

Hyacinth wrinkled her nose in disapproval. "That's creepy. Why would someone do such a thing?" She leaned down and Clyde poked his nose near Hyacinth's lace-gloved hand that matched the knee-high lace tights on her legs.

Caspen snaked an arm around Hyacinth's shoulder. His large, curly elf hair pulled back in a ponytail. He said his hello and he and Hyacinth left.

Terra hadn't gone far when a teen troll with two-toned yellow and green plumage walked into her path. Terra veered around her to keep up with Clyde and the troll spun on her heel and walked alongside her.

"Here." She handed Terra an envelope. She accepted the invitation as the troll continued to speak, "It's an invite to a party in Verboten tonight. You can bring the hunky warlock you hang out with too."

Tonight. Terra wanted to show Hank the antiquity room but, heck, it wasn't going anywhere. She'd show him another time. An invite was too good to pass up. Her fingers curled tight in a grip when she remembered how the elves dissed her when she first came to Provence by not inviting her. "Sure, sounds fun."

The troll's full lips formed a bountiful smile and her brown eyes twinkled as her tail plumage did a shake. "Perfect!"

Finally worn-out, Clyde rode on Terra's shoulder as they returned to the school. The invite was for after hours – ten p.m. There was plenty of time for dinner, a shower. She had no idea what to wear to a troll party, but guessed anything would work. It wasn't like they wore special attire, except she still wondered about their tails. Did their pants have holes?

She was really excited to get invited. There were no pureblood trolls in her friend group, nor in most of her classes as most were specific to elf magic. This would give her a chance to make her acquaintance with some. She wondered if Warlita would be there.

She was in mostly troll classes as she had more troll than anything, so she had to know at least a few. If they invited Terra, certainly they invited Warlita.

Hank pushed off one of the thick columns in front of the school he was leaned against. "I was thinking we could go for a walk tonight instead of practicing."

"I have something better," she responded as they walked in stride together towards the large double doors with pickaxe handles. "We've been invited to a party in Verboten."

He raised a brow. "They invited both of us?"

"Uhm hum," she mumbled, not giving him the satisfaction of knowing he was specifically requested to be there.

He reached a hand around the large pickaxe door handle and opened it for her. "You sure they invited me too?" he asked, as if he couldn't believe it. True, as a warlock, he wasn't well liked but people were coming around. He wasn't like other warlocks and had nothing to do with their invasion.

"That's what I said." She shot the sarcastic comment his way. He gave her a nasty glance, then they parted. Sometimes it bothered her that she couldn't always be nice to him. Understanding herself better than anyone, she knew it was her desire for him and lack of wanting involvement, combined with destiny's strange twist of forcing them together. She'd never been one to be told she had to do something and generally fought against it.

At dinner, she didn't say anything about the party to anyone, except Warlita who, as she suspected, was invited too. She would meet up with Terra and Hank and the three of them would go together. The hard part would be making an excuse to Halsey, who no doubt would ask questions. Terra got lucky there too.

Since Halsey started dating Bjorn, she had late nights occasionally. This happened to be one of them. As Hank, Warlita, and Terra carefully maneuvered their way down the two flights of stairs, they decided to go out a back door through the gym instead of prancing out the front.

They hadn't made it too far when Terra spotted Bjorn's lime sherbet colored hair, his arms sliding down Halsey's light blue dress, their lips locked tighter than a secure biometric safe. Even a locksmith couldn't pry them apart. Clyde walked alongside Terra on his harness and even he paused at the sight. Neither Halsey nor Bjorn noticed as they slipped past them.

She didn't think she could ever get tired of the beauty in Verboten. The pinks and purples, green and blue ribbons that moved through the sky like water. The colors shone against the gemstones poking up from the soil. Each realm had its own character. Fluffy feathers poked up from the ground as the folibees slept. They were large, ostrich-like birds with colorful tail feathers, much like the plumage trolls had on their tails. At night, they folded their legs and curled their heads to their chests so their feathers were all one could see.

REALM WALKER

Clyde ran ahead, as he did the night she snuck into Aradia with her hot fugitive friend, Tania, who she'd saved from Blood River in Drakonia. Occasionally, her mind still wandered to Tania and how she was faring in Lols, harvesting souls. The moments they shared still fresh in Terra's mind, along with her feelings for her, another factor that made it hard to be with Hank.

"I hear music," Warlita said, as she skipped ahead with Clyde.

Within a few moments, in the thick of the trees were more troll teens than Terra had ever seen. Some were seated on large gemstones, others milling around.

"You made it!" said the troll who handed Terra the invitation. Her eyes gave Hank a not-so-quick study as they slid up and down his fine, warlock body, studying his muscular curves more than Terra thought appropriate. A bite of green jealousy nipped at Terra's heart as the troll's two-toned plumage rubbed against Hank's arm. At that moment, she wanted to wrap her arms around him and smother him in a wet kiss to mark her territory. Instead, she squeezed his hand.

He gritted his teeth and wiggled his hand. Realizing she was squeezing the blood from his hand, she loosened her grip. The whole time wearing a tense smile.

They were a thing, kind of. Whatever was between them both frightened and excited her, leaving her all kinds of confused. His warm hand in hers sent tingles over her spine as they followed the bubbly teen to a long gemstone with a couple drink dispensers filled with a glowing blue fluid. The troll grabbed a disposable cup, filling it with the glowing blue drink and handing it to Hank.

Taking the drink, he shot a side glance at Terra who inhaled deeply and let out a long blast of air to keep from saying or doing something she'd regret later. Hank liked her. He'd made that clear with his nonstop chasing and occasional stolen kiss in her weak moments, like the electrifying firework provoking one at the new minister's celebration in Drakonia.

"Thanks," Terra stated almost mechanically when the girl handed her a drink.

"We call it eclipse ice. Don't drink it too fast. It's made from fermented buttons - the circular moss that grows on trees. It'll mess you up real quick."

Terra glanced around for Warlita and spotted her with a group of trolls she assumed she knew from school.

The girl took the cup from Hank's hand and placed it on the table. Giving Terra a brown-eyed glance, she said, "Will you watch that? I'm stealing him for a dance."

Anger and jealousy flew up Terra's spine. *Was she here just to bring him? Was that it?*

Hank gave her a wink, no doubt enjoying the jealousy flaming in Terra's eyes, as he followed the troll to the middle where everyone was dancing between the trees. It was lucky she'd learned control of magic or she might breathe angry fire and burn the forest down. The troll's skirt flared as she danced. Terra took several deep breaths to stay calm.

Throughout the night, Terra barely had more than a moment with Hank. The troll who invited her was only the first of a line of troll teens who stole his attention and practically drooled over him all night.

"They do that," a male troll said as he plopped on a gemstone next to Terra. His light hair shining pink from the ribbons in the sky above them.

"What?"

"He's the new guy. Girls always like the new guy."

True. Probably why her best friend back home in San Francisco was a male; a gay male. She missed Noah. It was her own fault. Since blasting the invaders back to Lols and sealing the veils she hadn't stepped foot in Lols and she missed it. "Yeah."

Swallowing the last drop of the third sweet and icy blue drink, the trees swam around Terra and she fell over a stone. Her butt landing on the side of it, she slid off, feet in the air.

The boy rushed to her and reached for her hands, his blue plumage pointing straight up in the air.

A fit of laughter caught her and she couldn't stand.

"How many of those have you had?" he asked, pointing to the cup still in her hand.

"Thr…eeeee," she said between chuckles.

He nodded, a knowing glance in his eyes. When her chuckles subsided, he again tried to help her up. This time she was able to stand.

The drink having its effect on her, she stared at the ribbons in the sky, "I want to touch them," she said, reaching her hand above her head. Like magic, the ribbons moved towards her, until her body buzzed with energy.

"Terra!" Terra!" someone yelled at her. Taking her mind off the ribbons moving through her hand, she stared into Hank's dreamy eyes. He stood above her. "We need to go."

"But the sky. I touched it."

In a panicked voice Hank asked, "Where's Clyde?"

She glanced around but didn't see him anywhere. Terror gripped her stomach and she forgot all about the sky ribbons. "Clyde!"

Warlita, bracelets dangling and clinking together, joined Terra who was screaming Clyde's name as she stumbled around trying to find him. "He's here. You were a little buzzed so I took him with me to meet a few new people. I hope that's OK."

Terra narrowed her eyes. "No, it's never OK to kidnap someone's pet…" As the words rolled off her tongue she fell on Warlita and passed out.

4

erra peeled an eye open as Clyde rooted beneath the covers. She pulled him into a grasp. He squirmed away as she rolled over. The curtains still drawn, she couldn't tell if the fake Provence sun was out. Carefully, she sat up in bed. Clyde poked his head out of the covers and sniffed at her chin.

Her brain ran in circles trying to remember the previous night. She recalled getting to Verboten, all the troll girls hanging all over Hank. Jealousy cropped up at the memory and she pushed it down. That was about all she remembered except the troll's warning not to drink too many eclipse ices.

"Ugh," she muttered, knowing she'd overdone herself.

It was one thing to drink her father's beer or sneak his expensive liquor, but another to drink too many alcoholic beverages made from who knows what in a foreign realm. She raised her knees and planted her head between them in embarrassment. *What did I do?*

Other than shame, she felt fine and wasn't nursing a hangover. She pushed the covers back and parted the curtains. It was daytime. Good thing it was day five and she didn't have classes. A knock on the door made her jump.

Collecting herself, she opened the door. Hank stood there with a crooked smile on his face, his jeans hanging just right, and the sleeves of his plain dark blue T-shirt teased to show the rune tattoos on his upper arm. They made her want to do nasty things with him. She leaned against the door frame.

"Good morning, sunshine. How do you feel?"

"Better than I look... Did I...? What did I...?" she stumbled to get the words out.

His eyes moved over her body. She glanced down, realizing all she was wearing was a long T-shirt and underwear. *Crap!*

"You look pretty good." His dark eyes twinkled with his dirty thoughts.

"Give me a minute." She pushed the door closed, leaving him in the hallway.

After pulling on clothes, running a brush through her straight hair and over her teeth, she reemerged.

They talked as they walked. She'd gotten so high, or drunk, or whatever it was, on the eclipse ice that she'd literally started pulling the sky down. Her face turned all shades of red and Hank chuckled.

"It's not funny!"

He pinched his fingers together. "It is, just a little."

She hated all the power she had. This proved she couldn't be a normal teen. No! She had to be realm walker teen with an abundance of power that she had barely tapped into and just when she felt she was beginning to control it. No, it controlled her. "Whatever." She pushed a hand against his chest and walked ahead of him. Clyde scampered alongside her.

A hand touched her shoulder and she swung around to Hank. "Listen, when I first started to develop powers I didn't know what to do with them. I still don't understand the rune I got when we first…" His words dropped off.

Kissed. That's what he was going to say.

"There's something remarkable and powerful between us and that rune has everything to do with it, but I don't know what it means other than what..." His words trailed off to avoid sticking his foot in his mouth again and mentioning M'ra. Terra's heart was still tender at the mention of her name.

Being around him was intoxicating and frightening. They'd had that talk after their kiss in Drakonia. The energy between them was great and with it they could do anything, including harm. As much as she forced herself to believe that, she knew it was much more and, after last night, getting drunk and pulling the sky down, she was more terrified of the power.

Hank had been great. He hadn't pushed her but allowed her the time she needed to sort through the wildness in her brain. Time to process and learn to command magic. When they trained, she was in control, but when they kissed she lost that control.

"Don't you have a guide or book that explains all the runes?"

"No, we have no written word of our past, who we are, the runes, nothing, because it is part of our culture to stay hidden amongst the humans, but there's someone who's been helpful." His face gave away that she might not approve and she gave him the spit it out look. "Jukane."

The new minister of Drakonia. How on earth did he know anything about warlocks? "Jukane. So now you're on a first name basis with the new minister of Drakonia?" *Why did she even question it?* At the celebration, after the minister accepted the ring and all the responsibility that went with it, he set her up with Hank. Even though Hank helped her save the realm, there were those who were skeptical of him being a warlock. It was his kind that killed the previous minister and other vampires with their sunlight runes.

They reached the cafeteria and she grabbed Clyde and stuck him up her baggy shirt in case the dragon cafeteria lady was around. That wasn't a confrontation she needed again in her life. "Can you warm me an egg and bacon croissant? I'm going to the courtyard."

Understanding Clyde wasn't supposed to be in the cafeteria, Hank nodded. Terra sat at the same table she'd been sitting at with her friends since coming to Provence. The tables empty as they were late for the show, as she usually was on day five unless she had a pressing matter. She looped Clyde's leash around the back of her stool and smoothed her hands against the colorful abalone-like tiles on the table. Hank returned carrying a tray with a huge bowl of cereal, her sandwich, and a couple of drinks.

Hank didn't waste time in picking up the conversation where they'd left it, explaining his relationship with the vampire minister as if he had to justify it. "Jukane was good to me when the other vampires weren't." He dipped his spoon into the bowl of flake cereal. "He's grateful. I helped him. M'ra sent spies to Earth that she called intercepts but there was a flaw with the plan. Human vampires can walk in the day, Darkonian vampires can't. Each vampire returned for the ceremony and we sent them back with the daylight spell."

Hank never referred to the human realm as Lols and never called humans commoners. She admired that, even though his words stung like wasps. She lowered her sandwich, her mouth turning downward. She had no idea M'ra had sent spies and Hank hadn't thought to tell her this until now. She felt the warmth rise in her cheeks. "Why did you keep this from me?"

A pained look shone in his dark eyes. The fake sun high in the sky shed no warmth and she suddenly felt cold. If it had been real she would have felt its heat on her head. Her feelings weren't justified, she knew that, yet her heart dropped in her chest as if she'd been betrayed. She'd upset him.

Sadness flashed in his eyes. "Don't misplace your anger on me. It was the vampires – M'ra – who kept that from you. You may be a realm walker, and the only one, but that doesn't entitle you to know everything and run each realm." His words snapped and snarled with anger that didn't rear its ugly head often in him.

Did she feel entitled? Was the power going to her head? No, she knew herself well. This was how she acted when she was hurt and she was misplacing her anger. He'd called it. M'ra was one of the first realm walkers and a direct ancestor, as her line donated DNA to Cyrus who was her biological father. Terra shared that connection with her and no one else and had thought of M'ra as far more than the minister of Drakonia – a motherly figure she'd never had. "You're right. I'm sorry."

He dropped the spoon in his bowl and pushed his hands across the table, covering hers. Warm tingles raced from her hands to her heart. "I get it. You're alone. When M'ra was alive you weren't. I'm alone too. That's why I spelled the vampires to walk in the daylight. I have to make my own alliances. You have that, even though you don't see it."

Why was he right? She hated herself in that moment. All she'd been through the last several months was overwhelming, but she'd always landed on her feet.

"Your friends. Each one would do anything for you. Most days I don't know where I stand in your life. This connection between us is strong and, like it does you, it scares me and I don't have a single warlock to turn to and ask about it."

Guilt hung heavy in her heart. She hadn't considered how alone he was. The fact he couldn't go home was tragic but she couldn't either, not permanently, and yet the last few months, he'd been patient. Never asked about the stones, about going to Marsidia, or returning to Lols to find the exit stones. He hadn't pushed because he, like her, was unsure of the present and the future.

"Am I an alliance too?" She kicked herself mentally as soon as the words left her mouth. Why didn't she think before she spoke? Or was it her shield to protect herself from her true feelings for him and insecurities in the power she contained? The pulse that rhythmically beat inside her. There was something strong that ached and begged for her yet she fought the connection because, the last time she used it in Drakonia, it scared her and she wasn't willing to admit that to anyone. She barely accepted it herself, yet it ruled her every action.

"No! I don't know what you are. I only know I'm bound to you and I can't get you out of my head."

She changed her course and allowed the empathy she felt for him. He was alone except for her. Minister Jukane had become a friend to him, and the group she met through Kinzo and the ones she brought from Lols had become friends to her. "Tell me about Marsidia."

He swallowed a bite of cereal, barely chewing, as she figured it was probably plenty soggy by now. "The stories have been passed verbally for centuries. I'm not even sure if they are true but it's always described as a place with grass made of gold, sheets of color spread across the sky more beautiful than the aurora borealis. Woods fill the lands with leaves in warm shades of purple and blue. Below the hills are grassy lands that lead to the valley and the source. It's sentient and wise."

The blob, as Terra thought of it. The painting under the palace in Navarin showed the blob and spheres hurtling towards it, then an explosion, then the Serenity Tree and life. It was Hank who interpreted it, but it was only a hypothesis. "It sounds really beautiful." The next words out of her mouth caught her by surprise and she cursed her limited brain-to-speak filter. "We will get there."

"I've always dreamed of going there... I haven't been completely honest with you."

Here it came. If Jukane and spies weren't enough, there was more. Instead of getting fired up she stayed calm. "About?"

Running a hand over the top of his head, he explained the rune that shone the day they first tried using magic together grows each time they touch. Most runes were written in their language which, to Terra, was a bunch of weird lines that didn't make any sense. The one on his thigh was a series of symbols.

She sighed, having no idea what that could mean. Phantom stabbing pains mocked her chest where the passports formed. One for each realm. The rune had brought him pain too and Clyde's warm breath reduced the pain, the same as it had done for the passports. Were they connected somehow? "Did it hurt?"

He nodded, as if her expression gave away the thoughts in her mind. "Yes, but no more than normal runes when they appear. That day when we touched, that rune was more painful than any, almost like someone was carving it with a knife."

The spell that created realm walkers and the veils between the realms was powerful. Based on her limited understanding, Merla's spell wasn't original. She'd concocted it from a previous spell. It made her brain hurt to think too long about the secrets of their ancestors. Was there more to the spell, something sinister?

Her thoughts went to the antiquity room. Now wasn't the time, as she didn't want to get caught, but tonight, after lights out. "I haven't been honest with you either," she admitted. "I wasn't trying to be dishonest." Her words circled as she finally spit them out. "I have something to show you tonight."

5

The elf stylist asked, "What do you think?" and handed Terra a gold filigree mirror.

Giving it a good look: Straight bangs lay neatly against her forehead and the sides fell in front of her ears and past her chin, the back trimmed neatly at the hairline. Layers gave it body and depth, absorbing the pinks and golds of Sizzle Cuts. Brown chunks lay beneath her on the floor. "I feel like myself again."

Chella, the elf stylist, smiled. "I aim to please. The colors and tones are so unique they should never be hidden." She winked as she pulled the cutting gown off Terra.

She always felt the same way about her hair. Its blended tones taking on any color. She guessed it was what made realm walkers blend into whichever realm they resided in.

Hank stood from the stone bench as she exited the shop in Provence Square, his jeans crinkled above the thighs. She guessed he'd been waiting for her awhile. A slanted smile crossed his lips. "I like it. It fits you better."

Clyde chased the shadow of the setting fake sun, his harness fitted around him. Hank unwound the leash and passed it to Terra.

"Thanks for watching him."

He shrugged. "Clyde and I have something to show you," he said, walking around the corner of Sizzle Cuts as it was an end unit. Taking Clyde's leash, she walked with him.

That evening, her mind wandered to Provence. She looked at it with a different set of eyes. In the inbetween, she created her own space. That's what Provence was, a creation of realm walkers and the spell. Marya's journal explained how it was once a treacherous land filled with unspeakable dangers but, when she and Matthia crossed it after the spell was complete, it was similar to what it is now – a safe space for all.

The Ring of Betrayal

She wouldn't have used such an annoying scent, and certainly would have added a breeze. The still air drove her nuts, but she appreciated the imagination it took to create the space. Since learning her powers and returning from Drakonia she'd thought many times about how she'd change it, like remodeling a home, but considered against it as it would certainly draw attention to herself.

The tribunal agreed not to punish her. They weren't as forgiving as each realm leader and hadn't showered her with presents but did give her a pass. After all, it wasn't her fault she was what she was. That was the fault of her parents. The tribunal didn't know who her real father was. She felt if they did she wouldn't have been given a pass. To her, he donated sperm and physical traits but not character. The father who raised her did that.

"Right there between the trees," Hank said as he ducked below a hanging branch filled with purple leaves.

A blanket lay over the grass set up with a basket. "What's this for?" she asked, overwhelmingly surprised.

"We train all the time, eat with your friends, but outside of that we don't spend much time together. We have a strong connection and, after our talk earlier, I think we need to nurture it more and try and understand what it means."

REALM WALKER

It was a sweet, romantic gesture, and one that amplified his interest in her. Avoiding him is what she did and practice with him appeased her want for him. She'd pushed back her jealous feelings from the previous night. They were a knee-jerk reaction, but she had no claim on him nor him on her. Destiny said otherwise.

The fake sun dropped in the faux sky as they spent time together, not discussing their feelings or practicing magic, but simply being with each other. As a former commoner, he brought all the right foods: sandwiches, chips, fruit, and soda. It was a human thing, a commoner thing.

Stuffing the last bite of a honey ham sandwich into her mouth, she played with the strawberries and pulled the stems off.

Hank snapped his fingers and a glowing ball appeared between them, hovering over the basket. She stuffed a strawberry in her mouth, its juices showered her tongue as she savored the sweet delight.

He tossed a strawberry into the air and caught it in his mouth. Terra smiled. Pulling the stem off another, he brushed it against her lips and she snatched it between her teeth. After emptying his bottle of soda in a few gulps, he tossed it into the basket and lay down.

In the short time they'd known each other, they'd undergone a wild adventure, saved the realms, learned they were fated or mated, or whatever. She consciously worked against it. But she didn't know much about him.

Having finished her food, she leaned back on the blanket and stared at the fake stars. They didn't even twinkle. "Tell me about your family, about you."

"My parents are underperforming warlocks, so I grew up like any human in suburbia with three little brothers: fourteen, ten, and six. They have mundane jobs, pay the bills, and escort my brothers to their little league games."

That was a start. Not really what she was hoping for. "What about you?"

"I went to warlock school, like every warlock, and showed promise. I think my parents like being average. For me, either I showed skill or I went back home to repeat my parents' boring life. I think my parents prefer not drawing attention to themselves. My father has this rune that allows him to wrap anything in silver, but he keeps it hidden. I had to show I was worth a chance, although I never understood the regional wizard's interest in me. My runes are basic, except this one I got after I met you that connects me to the source, but she called me in for an assignment that led me to you."

He'd already told Terra energy follows her and he can see it. According to him, he never told anyone else. "Tell me about her."

He blew air out of his cheeks like he didn't know where to start. "She's powerful, intimidating, and hates werewolves. Most warlocks hate werewolves. They're crude, unlike the more refined vampires. I hated being called in front of her. It made me nervous."

Terra'd had her run ins with powerful women. They were wholly scarier than powerful men because women were also conniving, and men were straightforward and weak. Inferior, in many ways, to women.

He reached for her hand, cupping his fingers around it, and brought their folded hands into the air. His hand so much larger than hers, it swallowed it in silky skin. "What about you?"

"I grew up with my dad. It was always me and him. He never remarried. I have no siblings unless I count Noah, my lifetime across the street neighbor and best friend. We shared all our important moments together, our anxieties, crushes, and often slept at each other's homes."

Hank's face a combination of concern and confusion, Terra clarified. "He's 100% gay." *And he'd eat you up!* She kept those words to herself as she let out a small giggle. "In kindergarten he didn't chase girls for a kiss, he chased boys."

"You miss him."

She brushed her thumb along his. "I miss my life. Magic is new to me. I didn't grow up with it, never knew my dad was a dragon. When I think about it now, our RV trips across the country to the most remote areas make sense. Growing up, it was adventure. It's how Clyde became part of the family." Hearing his name, Clyde bounded towards Terra and crawled over her chest.

Hank stretched his long legs then wiggled them as Clyde climbed over one leg then the other. "Sometimes I think Marsidia might look a lot like Provence."

The teal daylight sky gone, it still carried a blueish hue. Her mind still considering the stars, she thought to make them twinkle and they did. Was that part of a realm walker's duty? To improve on what was already. The ball of light Hank created hovered between them.

He brought her hand to his chest, every beat of his heart thrumming against her wrist, the blanket between them. The stars moved into a constellation she didn't recognize. "What is that?"

"My parents never taught us much about Marsidia. The basics. They taught us the language, but more out of fear of not being 'warlock enough' than wanting us to claim who we are. At warlock school is where I learned what I know…" He leaned his head towards Terra, his velvety brown eyes meeting hers. "It's a group of stars in Marsidia above the source."

The group of stars formed what looked like a series of letters; a Y shape, a diamond with two legs, and a backwards Z, all connected. "What does it mean?"

He shrugged. "I don't know. It's not in our language and is mostly legend, but some say it means destiny, others say it means renewal; the circle of life and death."

Studying the strange lines, zags, and shapes, it didn't look like anything really. "Maybe it's a tangled mess of coincidence." The Warlock language and runes covering parts of his body, similar to the old fae language, were a series of wavy lines crossing each other.

He leaned upward on an elbow, his braids puddling on the sheet around his arm. "Runes never mean nothing. This is the rune that connects us and our powers."

To avoid the subject as if it was a semi-truck, she maneuvered the conversation. "Its time." Standing on her feet, she offered him a smile and picked up Clyde who was happy to ride on her shoulder.

Guilty needles stabbed at her spine for not allowing the romantic night to take a more romantic turn and ease her desires for him.

Bringing Hank to the antiquity room had a dual purpose. She was curious about the object that had a clutch on Clyde. Alex said it spoke, but she hadn't heard it. Sometimes she forgot all the ways she could mold and play with magic and hadn't thought to listen.

Hank's eyes widened as they took in all the stuff. It was a hoarder's dream room and she didn't know what most of the stuff did. "There might be history of your people here or their relationship with others."

"What is all this?" he asked as he picked up a metal candelabrum.

She groaned and ordered, with a sharpness to her voice, "Put that down. This is all magical stuff. I don't know what most of it does. There are scrolls over there." She pointed to the baskets along the wall, thinking they were safe enough.

While he studied the scrolls, unrolling them and stretching them out, she unlocked the box that held the metal feather pen. Lifting the lid, she studied the pen and listened with her realm walker ears. Its message one she didn't understand. It was old fae by the sounds of it, or a different ancient language.

Hank was reading an unrolled scroll as she approached with the box. "You have a rune that allows you to hear things right. Listen to this."

He nodded and glanced at the box. "I thought you said not to touch things."

"I did. You also asked about Clyde. He had the thing in this box in his mouth. Alex said it was enchanted and speaking to him, but he couldn't understand what it was saying. I don't understand the language —"

He cut her off. "You think I can."

She offered him a cheesy smile. Of course, he understood warlock and, subsequently, old fae.

"Anything for Clyde and you…" His voice drifted off as he laid the scroll down and collected the box. "It's warlock and says for us to meet at Mer Point in Navarin. The sound waves are high pitched and a level only animals hear, unless you have magic that allows you to hear the pitch. Clyde was meant to find it."

Clyde was an animal. Why target an animal? Then it clicked. "It was meant for me. Clyde was the conduit. Whoever sent it knew I'd figure it out. When?"

He lowered his brows. "No, my job is to be your guardian. You can't go running off into trouble. If you do this, we do this and have a plan first."

Terra pressed a hand on her hips. She hadn't thought of doing it alone. Yes, she had grown her command of magic but was still in her infancy with it. She was far stronger with Hank. "I didn't plan on doing it alone," she snapped.

"You run into things headfirst without thinking through it."

Even though he was right, his words upset her. "That was the old me."

He dropped it. "I'll go check it out, first."

She chuckled. "You so easily forget I can see every realm." *Except the inner realm of Marsidia,* she thought, taking pains not to say that out loud. "We'll go together."

6

Terra found it hard to concentrate in class as she attempted to use her mind to have a conversation with a tree. That's what they did in Plant Connections. They talked to plants. Her one-way conversations had blossomed into actual communications. Some plants had a sense of humor, others didn't – like the one she was talking with now.

It's easier to have a conversation with someone who has coherent thought, sniped the silver-leafed Fryca tree.

Terra apologized, as her thoughts were everywhere.

The Ring of Betrayal

We are always with you. The one who calls you doesn't wish to harm you, the tree explained in a smooth stream of thought.

What does he or she want?

I'm not sure, but your help, I feel.

Help? What could Terra offer? Fae weren't the nicest subspecies.

They're not, but this one isn't full fae, the Fryca tree revealed, responding after having read her thoughts.

"You've come such a long ways," Terra's instructor noted as she sat cross legged across from Terra, her long, dark hair in a Dutch braid that flowed onto the grass.

Terra offered her instructor a smile. "I'm learning, but have problems centering my thoughts," she said, thinking of her conversation with the Fryca.

"Close your eyes, feel the plant's smooth leaves, the grain of its stem or trunk, the newness of its blooms."

Terra closed her eyes and reached with her mind to the Fryca, but was quickly bombarded with flowers opening their petals and several textures of leaves, stems, and bark. Colors exploded in her mind and suddenly a flurry of conversations overwhelmed her. She squeezed her eyes in an attempt to focus on one at a time and found herself conversing with several plants at a time. Her mind focused and in harmony with the flora surrounding her.

"You see," her instructor said with a knowing smile as Terra opened her eyes and saw Hank standing against a tree waiting for her. Clyde circled her, the leash on his harness tying her legs together. Class over, she pried her legs free and joined Hank, anxious to get to Navarin and the not-pureblooded fae that beckoned her.

Tall, fine blades of golden grass bent over from the steady breeze of the lavender sea below. Mer Point was a ledge that hung over a sea foam sandy beach. She walked to the edge and glanced down. The clear lavender water sparkled with fairy dust and bioluminescent organisms. Further away, she noted the massive showy tails of the sea fae, the mer people, and remembered Meesha's words about their scales containing a poisonous toxin.

Terra had seen her friend Kayln in her sea fae form. If she hadn't been so preoccupied that day, she'd have noted how beautiful and impressive her mer form was.

Hank joined Terra as he'd tagged further behind. It was his first trip to Navarin. "Look." He pointed as a pink tail splashed above the water, creating bioluminescent, sparkly waves that crashed along the shore.

"Navarin has its own charm," Terra admitted, even though the nippy energy had all her nerve endings standing at attention in annoyance.

"It's the most breathtaking of all the realms, except maybe Marsidia," a female voice, one she least expected, responded to their conversation.

Terra spun around. Terina stood a few feet away. The sea fae/warlock who used the rip in the veil of her home to steal fairy dust and spell the pastries she sold at her bakery – A Slice of Pie. She'd stolen the enter Stones of Hovrath, but luckily Terra and Hank had retrieved them.

Terra didn't agree with Terina's biased perception of Navarin. All the realms were beautiful. The elven realm of Aradia had its colorful forest and mysterious darklands. Canida, land of the lycans, had its prairies and wildflowers. Sier, the dragon realm, was one of her favorites with its glowing stones and shiny metals that covered the caves and cities built into the highlands. The vampire realm of Drakonia even had its own beauty once she got over the scent of death. Its cities were built along Blood River, made from the blood of harvested souls.

The troll realm of Verboten looked a lot like forests and clearings in Lols, except it had gemstones and precious metals as rocks sticking up from the ground and streams and ribbons of color in the sky. Thraves, similar to Sier, had cities built into the midlands as well as cities above the midlands. Inside the caves were glowing stalactites. She didn't argue

Terina's view as she was learning to control her tongue. "What do you possibly want from us?"

Terina's gaze shifted to Clyde, who sat on Terra's shoulder, then Hank. A smirk played on her lips. "Pretty clever messaging, right?"

Terra almost blew a gasket. Her messaging could have hurt Clyde. It had him under a spell. Leave it to a fae.

Hank, sensing Terra's rise in anger, emphasized Terra's words, "What do you want?"

"To go home."

What? Last they saw her she was home in Lols, hiding the Stones of Hovrath in a box in an underground dug out. After, Terra and Hank blasted the warlocks, wolves, and vampires from Lols back to Lols. Centering her thoughts, she'd found with fae it wasn't always wise to play all the cards and kept her temper in check. "Why would we do that?"

Terina played with her nails as she gazed beyond them at the lavender sea. "I'm not full fae and… have lived in secret, hiding in the shadows for months. I've overheard things from others who hide in the shadows."

"What kind of things?" Hank asserted, narrowing his eyes.

"If I tell you, you have to send me home."

Terra's eyes met Hank's and they made a visual agreement of sorts. "I'll send you home if the information is good, otherwise you can stay here."

Freckles danced in desperation as Terina quickly said, "Deal."

According to Terina, there were whispers carried in sound waves few could hear that were looking for the Stones of Hovrath. "They call themselves the Council of Divination. The plan is to acquire the stones and destroy the realm walker and the…" she stumbled over the words, finally she spat them out, "realms."

Their faces unclear, as the ability to hear and see them was something new for Terina, something she felt was part of her warlock and happening because of her stay in Navarin.

Hank raised an eyebrow, a strong sea breeze catching his thick braids and pushing them over his shoulders. "You're a dreamer."

"A what?" Terina asked.

"You're closer to the source and your warlock magic. Do you have a new mark?"

She nodded and lifted her shirt an inch above her waist. "This appeared a couple weeks after I was locked into the realms," she said with a testy tone.

Terra didn't feel any guilt. She didn't understand how she was still there, but didn't care. She understood that when warlocks gained a new power they'd get a mark like a brand, called a rune. "What is this dreamer thing?" Terra asked, wondering if they could make more use of it before sending her back.

"I see dreams, but these shadow people are like dreams and I can't figure out if I'm seeing their dreams or if that's the state they exist in," she said, her tone sincere.

Terra certainly didn't have that answer. "Do they know I have the enter Stones of Hovrath?"

She shook her head in a no. "But you must keep them safe and hidden."

Terra had them somewhere no one could look. She was the only one, as the only realm walker, who could enter the inbetween and the secret little place she'd designed. In the trunk of a tree, with everything else she didn't want others to find, such as Merla's Realm Grimoire and the pure soul she'd found in Thraves.

If they were going to make a deal, she was greedy and wanted the exit stones too. According to Hank, there were enter and exit stones to Marsidia. As a pair they were the Stones of Hovrath. If she and Hank were ever going to Marsidia, they needed both stones. As much as she'd been avoiding it, she couldn't avoid it forever. Their destinies were interwoven and had something to do with Marsidia, the source, and who knew what else.

She swallowed the lump in her throat. "Do you have the exit stones?"

Terina lowered her head. "I lied when I said I had them. My father hid them, but I don't know where. They could be anywhere, hidden in anything."

Terra wasn't sure if she believed her. According to Hank, Terra'd touched them in the professor's storage room of hoarded magical and historical treasures, but Terina wouldn't know that. She tended to believe her, even though she betrayed them in the past. "What more do you know about them?"

"My dad was clever. They'll be disguised and probably hidden in plain sight. You won't be able to feel their energy. He'll have disguised that too."

That wasn't much help. Someone stole them from the storage unit, but it did explain how they were hidden for so long. "You help us find the exit stones and I'll send you back to Lols."

"They aren't in Navarin, and I can't enter any other realm. Send me home and I'll look for them there."

Terra folded her arms over her chest. It made sense that they were in Lols, but who took them? Her gut said they were in one of the realms. "I can send you into any realm and disguise you." It was a tall order, as Terra wasn't great with transformation, but she didn't let on.

REALM WALKER

Terina rolled her eyes and reluctantly whined, "Deal."

The warlock's only goal seemed to be getting home to Marsidia, which meant having the Stones of Hovrath. When they invaded, the werewolves came to Verboten, the vampires to Navarin, and the warlocks to Aradia. At first, Terra thought it was to surround Navarin, but now she was thinking maybe it was more. The enter stones were in Navarin but no one knew what they did, the history lost or hidden beneath the palace where the fae took her and Hank.

She found them by chance because she'd read Marya's journal 'The Origin' and knew the disturbance was colorful like the stones. It had been an educated guess on her part that panned out. She would send Terina into the other two realms.

"You start tonight in Verboten," Terra relayed. It was her chance to practice transforming someone else. M'ra was only able to transform and hold it for others in troll form. Terra, being a descendent, figured that was a good place to start and maybe the troll form would be easier on someone else. Verboten also seemed a logical choice, as trolls were known to be smiths and would have a natural curiosity for the Stones of Hovrath.

Hank slid her a disapproving glance from the corner of his eye. She didn't need his approval and she needed to hone her skill set better.

Terina let out an aggravated sigh.

Outside of Provence, they could use level 3 magic and Terra had gotten pretty good at portalling, as she used that method to go from one realm to the next. Huge gems appeared to grow out of the grass. Terina's eyes had dollar signs in them, but she wouldn't be allowed to take anything from the realm.

Transforming her into a troll wasn't too difficult, but holding all three of them as trolls took skill. She wouldn't have bothered transforming herself and Hank except they'd stand out if she didn't and, after the other night, she preferred to stay hidden.

With poofy purple tail plumage, Terina grumbled almost immediately, but not about her troll form: "I don't know the first place to look."

Terra mocked, "You said it would be hiding in plain sight."

Terina rolled her eyes. "What are we going to do? Lift every gemstone? Those things look heavy."

"No, you are," Terra spat, still not fond of the testy fae/warlock.

Hank sputtered as he attempted to hold in a laugh. No doubt he was amused by their banter. She dealt daily with the fae princess and knew how to handle the uppity breed.

Terra smoothed her hand against Hank's as they folded their fingers over the backs of their hands. Using their telepathic connection, she directed the magic to a large green stone. It wiggled then lifted up, shaking the ground, rising into the colorful atmosphere a few feet. It left a hole about a foot deep. Terra held in a chuckle.

Terina stumbled backwards and looked ready to run as her eyes grew wild and shifted from the rock to Terra's face then Hank's. Terra curled her fingers together and formed a bubble around them to contain Terina.

Ignoring Terina's ready to run expression and body language, Hank said calmly, "You don't need to physically look. Listen and watch. Use your dreamer rune. With it, you too can hide in the shadows."

Terina blinked a couple times then relaxed as they lowered the large gem. For Terra it was really a show of power to keep Terina in line.

"C'mon," Terra urged, following the walking trail through the trees that led to Rubina, the capitol. "The trolls are very democratic. They have an upper council of three elected leaders that make decisions for the realm, and a lower chamber with a mayor from every village. The capitol seems the best place to start." It was the highest probability that a politician would know the secrets of their realm and those thoughts might drift into their dreams.

The three walked into the city. Smooth gems and metals made the streets, the futuristic buildings built with other metals molded to form domes and various shapes. Terra's eye wandered as she'd never actually been to Rubina. Gwond, her magic instructor, always took her to the forest when they practiced level 3 magic. He'd paid special attention to her, as she was his only realm walker student and her command of magic was unlike any others.

"It's like something from a futuristic cartoon," Terina mumbled with a wandering eye.

Terra ignored her comment. Vehicles buzzed above them as trolls walked the gemstone-lined streets. She had no idea they were this advanced. "There." She pointed. "That's the capitol." Metallic steps led to an oval building that appeared made of gold.

Terra needed to get back to Provence or she'd stay and watch the fae/warlock. She had no trust in her, yet Terina couldn't escape Verboten on her own and, using magic to disguise her, Terra would know exactly where to find her through the connection. "I need to get back to Provence, but there's a small cottage outside Rubina. Follow the road we came in on and, when you see the tree with naked roots covered in gold, turn left. The path will take you there." She'd been there with Gwond, that's how she knew of it, and figured Terina would be safe enough there.

Terina squawked like a bird on drugs. "What? You're leaving?"

"Yeah, I'm a student. I have classes and homework. Find out what you can. I'll be back. Oh, and hide at night. I'm not sure if I'll be able to keep your form while I sleep."

Terina shook her head and grabbed Terra's arm. Hank did something Terra didn't expect. He placed a hand on Terina's arm. "You don't have permission to touch her."

It was so out of character. Sure, he was her *guardian* but also knew she was quite capable of taking care of herself and Terina was of little threat. "It's fine Hank," she said as she turned to Terina. "You've been hiding in the shadows, at least now you look like you fit."

7

The scent of Provence made Terra's nose twitch as they walked through the curtain. Level 3 magic not allowed in Provence, she portalled them to the curtain.

"I don't think she ever had the stones," Hank said.

His words didn't really surprise Terra. She'd thought the exact same thing but hadn't shared her thoughts with him. "Remind me."

He walked alongside her as they strolled back to Provence Academy. "That's how the warlocks learned of you. You awoke something dormant in a storage room, but it wasn't there when the warlocks went to retrieve it."

"You think it was the exit Stones of Hovrath?"

"Yes."

She thought back. She and her friends were sent to Lols to find five commoners to be diplomats for Lols. One of the people on their list was a college professor with a penchant for collecting ancient artifacts. There was one she'd knocked over. When she touched it, vibrations moved through her hand. It was shaped similar to a cross and was jeweled. It was cylindrical with two cones on the sides that met in the middle of the cylinder.

She pulled her phone out from her back pocket. It didn't make phone calls in any realm but Lols yet it still had uses – pictures. She'd gone back into the professor's storage unit and taken pictures. "Does it look like this?" She handed Hank her phone.

He stopped walking and pulled his fingers to the edges of the screen to zoom in. "That's it."

Words were etched into the metal in old fae, or so she thought at the time, but that was before she knew warlocks existed. "What does it say?"

He handed her the phone. "I can't tell you."

What? Why not?! "Sure you can. Isn't it written in warlock?"

His eyes dropped and appeared to stare at his shoes as he brushed a hand over his long braids. "It is." He lifted his gaze to meet hers. "But I can't read it to you. It's the spell that, with the stones, opens the curtain between Marsidia and another realm for one to exit."

His words spun in her head before the implications of them sunk in. He didn't trust her. Did the enter stones work the same way? That's why he didn't fuss over her having them. He knew they were safe and was probably waiting for her to trust him enough to give them to him or show him where they were. She wanted to ball up her fists and have a Halsey fit but stayed cool as the frigid breath of an ice dragon. "You've known that. Even if I wanted to I can't use the enter stones."

"Correct." His tone cold, emotionless.

Anger simmered inside her. "You don't trust me."

"I do, but that key belongs to the warlocks and I trusted them too."

What was that supposed to mean? Anger erupted. She couldn't keep her cool any longer and stomped off, leaving him alone at the tree line between the woods and the school. She wanted to destroy something, bring Provence crashing down, but that would do nothing. Instead she went to her room and sulked on her bed until Halsey entered.

"I like it! You look so much better," Halsey stated as she flung herself on Terra's bed and reached over, pressing a palm under the side of Terra's hair.

"Thanks," Terra managed to say with little emotion.

Halsey twisted her perfect pink lips. "I know we don't always get along but I am your roommate. I did find the scroll for you, never tattled on all the things you did before anyone knew you were a realm walker, or even knew what a realm walker was…" She let out a sigh that sounded painful. "What I'm trying to say is: I'm your friend and you can trust me."

Wow! That was a lot coming from Halsey, and she was right. Terra had used her, having the Diama of Navarin as a roommate had its benefits once they reached some form of silent agreement. But could she trust her with this? There was only one way to find out. "You're right. It's the artifact we stole from Navarin." She thought about that for a moment. In Navarin, the fae had stuffed her and Hank in a dungeon over the artifact, then had them read the walls in a deeper dungeon. "What do you know of it?"

"Not much. It was there for hundreds of years. No one questioned the disturbance. I didn't even know it was caused by an artifact trapped between realms."

"What, what did you just say?"

"I didn't know it was there."

No the other part. Terra tempered her words. "The part about realms."

"That I didn't know it was trapped between realms."

Was that it? It was trapped between realms. Why did that bother Terra? Hadn't she already known that on some level? No, she thought it opened a gateway to the other realms because she read Marya's journal.

Halsey smoothed the fabric of her skirt. "I might know someone who knows something."

8

The someone who Halsey knew wasn't a someone at all. It was an ancient tree in the mangroves. The palace behind her, she could barely see its white peaks. The tree was thousands of years old and had survived the Great War. When the ice dragons came in they killed most of the vegetation in Navarin, which maintained a year-round tropical climate. Over time, the vegetation grew back. She pushed the boat along with the current towards the middle.

The water, a deeper purple and so dark she couldn't see any fish in the water. Flora surrounded her and made the journey take longer as she had to dodge the many roots and duck to avoid the hanging branches with their round leaves. The mangroves grew denser the further she went until she could barely see the golden sky. In the tunnel of trees, their branches arching over her, she took a rest. Her arms tired from rowing.

Tiny, colorful birds chirped and flitted between the branches as if they were chiding her for being there. Halsey had warned her the journey would take her the entire day, so Terra came prepared. Unzipping her backpack, she first opened a small container of food she'd packed for Clyde and a small water bowl. He scurried down her back.

Opening a bag, she pulled out a turkey sandwich she made and an apple. The birds' songs and chirps kept her company as she rested her back against the edge of the boat she'd pulled into a spit of dirt. Clyde scampered to the other end of the boat and raised his chest and head into the air. He looked silly, like a figurehead carved into an ancient boat not a tiny one-man kayak in a Navarin mangrove.

After she finished eating, she shook the kinks out of her arms, thinking this would be a great time to use magic. She mentally pushed the kayak into the water and steered it forward. *Much better*, she thought. Clyde cocked his head and looked at her with a disapproving face. "I'm tired."

Realm Walker

He scampered towards her and nudged at the oar. Halsey didn't tell her she couldn't use magic. She'd need to anyways to wake up the tree. He nudged again and she reached for the oar but not before the plants above them dropped and wrapped their vining arms around her. She fought against them, pushing with her hands and kicking with her feet. "Let me go!" she shouted.

Unable to see exactly what was happening, she felt them moving her forward. "Let me go!" she screamed. Energy exploded around her and the vining branches blew high into the air.

Why are you trespassing, realm walker? A voice spoke into her head and giggles exploded from all over.

The kayak moved forward quickly. She glanced behind her to see branches pushing it toward a dark area. The canopy of leaves allowed little light as she coasted and stopped in front of a large figure, enough light behind her to see it was a tree. A series of webbing roots curved out of the water and willowy leaves parted, revealing a thick trunk.

Shadows moved around the tree's trunk and giggles sounded as if they were coming from the trunk itself. Terra squinted her eyes but couldn't make out more than dark shadows.

Curious about what was behind the tree, she didn't ask but continued to watch.

"I'm here to speak with the ancient mangrove tree that survived the Great War."

I am she. What is it you want from me?

"Only memories." A shadow darted from behind the tree and branches rustled. There was something there. A pungent odor pushed its way up her nostrils as a breeze swept from under the trees.

I have many of those, the tree said whimsically. *No one visits me here.*

"You aren't easy to get to." Terra thought about the tree's reaction to magic. Had she woken them with a startle or did they not appreciate magic? What were the giggling shadows? Trees didn't walk, not even in the realms. Clyde sniffed at the tree's trunk, then circled back as if spooked and slowly moved toward the trunk again. "I'm sorry I used magic. My arms were sore from rowing all day."

It's lonely here.

This was getting nowhere really fast. "Can you tell me about the disturbance?" She'd be here longer than all day if she didn't get to the point.

Once, there were hundreds like me. We lived in the lower realms until the fae shut the warlocks out. They pushed us into hiding.

"I'm sorry." The story was familiar. The fae did the same thing with the elvarin in the darklands of Aradia. "Hundreds of mangroves?" Terra asked.

No. Willowy branches became like hair and a face formed at the top of the trunk, while the middle of the trunk took on a human form as the roots straightened into legs and feet. Two thicker branches on the side of the trunk formed arms, and standing before Terra was a green, humanoid creature. *Dryad.*

Terra couldn't stop her eyes from popping wide open as the tree transformed. She was beautiful and her skin looked like the soft green velvet moss that grew on trees. If she hadn't watched her transform, she probably wouldn't have seen her, as she blended into the mangroves. It was the perfect place for someone like her to hide.

Dryads. Terra'd heard of them as myth and lore in Lols, but not here. As much as it shocked her, it didn't. An unexpected wave of heat flushed her cheeks and water welled in the corners of her eyes. "Why would they do that?"

"You're not here because you knew I was a dryad?" the green, plant-like dryad asked, no longer speaking telepathically, her lips a darker green than her skin.

She was correct, and now maybe the conversation would get somewhere. "No. I was told you might know something about the disturbance and the artifact that caused it."

The dryad chuckled. "Why would I know such a thing? I live in the mangroves, apart from the Navarin world. If they knew I existed, I'd have been dead centuries ago."

Terra's fae friends excluded, she really didn't like fae. It seemed the more stories she heard about them, the more evil stuff she learned. The first tear from her eye dropped. There was too much hate between subspecies. "I'm sorry to bother you and wake up all the trees."

"We don't get company much, please stay," said a small creature as it stepped out from behind the dryad. It wasn't more than a couple feet tall, with front and bottom rows of sharp, pointed teeth. Little wisps of hair sprung from the top of its head. Terra almost jumped backwards in the water, her eyes growing round like saucers as she took in the hideous creature. Low branches wiggled as more little hideous creatures stepped forward.

"I do know something, but you'll have to stay for dinner."

The small creatures looked as though they could make a meal of Terra. She wasn't keen on staying but, if she left now, she wouldn't learn what she came to learn. "I'll stay."

The dryad's face lit up and the small creatures rushed to Terra's legs and wrapped their arms around her. Clyde rose up on his back legs and watched the creatures.

Realm Walker

The creatures, she soon found out, were dark nymphs. They once lived in the area between the realms, what is now Provence. When Provence was formed from magic, the curtains and veils were created. They were separated from each other and trapped in realms apart from one another. The dark nymphs in Navarin hid in the mangroves after most of their kind stuck in Navarin were killed by the fae. Terra's anger towards the fae bubbled over. Yes, the nymphs were ugly and they stank like rotting flesh, but they were alive and forced out of their home. They deserved what every other life form deserved – life and a chance to survive.

It turned out the dryad didn't always live as a tree, but spent most of her youth in her dryad form. The mangroves hid them well and no one ventured into them, allowing her to live a solitary life with only the mangrove trees and nymphs as friends. The trees talked, but couldn't do all that she could, grounded to the soil by their roots, and so she let them sleep and she took on her tree form and slept with them for centuries, until recently.

The dark nymphs had stayed hidden, eventually making their way further into the mangrove where they used the dryad's large branches as shade, and her size to help conceal themselves. Separated, did they also live in the darklands of Aradia? Is that why

Marya and Davi were warned not to look left or right but straight ahead?

They were all lonely and could only tell her the artifact was thrown into the sea to hide it and keep the fae from using it. Subsequently, it diverted water to the Serenity Tree after the birth of the realm walkers. Of course, it made sense the dryad was a tree, she'd share a connection to other trees.

Terina used Terra to get it. Terra had thought it was because she was given the perfect opportunity, but maybe it was more. Even in ancient times, the lavender seas were full of sea fae. Why didn't a single one retrieve the artifact?

Prickles ran up her spine. Had she inadvertently harmed the Serenity Tree? "And now?"

The dryad's eyes grew soft and moist. She blinked her velvety green lids. "I haven't heard from Serenity in a while."

9

The warm water pouring over Terra's head felt like a dream. She returned to Provence the following day, but this time she used magic and portalled instead of rowing. The muscles in her arms were weak and would hurt for days. The warm water helped alleviate some of the pain. Sleeping in the mangroves wasn't the most comfortable but she didn't want to upset the dryad or the dark nymphs. It seemed their lives were filled with enough suffering. Maybe now they had each other and things would be better.

The dryad told her the story how she fled to the mangroves as a child and grew up alone with the trees. Her parents, slaughtered by the fae, never joined her. She never dared to enter the outside world, as surely they'd kill her too. The history of the realms and its people was filled with such sadness, it weighed heavy on Terra's heart.

She wanted to put an end to it but didn't know how. As a realm walker, her one job was to keep peace between the realms. *How?* There was so much hate and misery and she was the only realm walker. At that moment she felt small, tiny in comparison to the heaviness of her heart.

She emerged from the shower and dressed, happy Halsey wasn't there. Not that she would divulge the dryad's secret. No, it was safe with her and, one day, if she truly was worthy of being a realm walker, she'd see to it that those oppressed like herself, the dryad, the dark nymphs, and those of the darklands could live at peace in their respective realms. It was a deep dish, but she hoped one day to make it happen.

Clyde in his harness, she opened the door to step into the hall. Instead she opened the door to see Hank standing outside it. "What?" she asked, not hiding her anger and disappointment in him.

"I'm sorry." He pressed a hand against the door frame. "Can we talk?"

No! She wasn't ready. Everything always pointed to the fae, but what about warlocks? They weren't innocent. Slamming the door in his face, she locked it and stepped back then broke a cardinal rule. She sliced the matter in the room open and stepped into the inbetween, coming out in Verboten. Level 3 magic wasn't allowed, nor was anyone other than her capable of using it in Provence. She'd respected the rule until now and felt a tinge of guilt for doing it. What no one else knew wouldn't hurt.

She'd brought him to the antiquity room. Showed him all the artifacts. That was something she didn't need to share. She did it hoping there was something present, maybe the stones.

The cottage she'd sent Terina to wasn't more than a small, modular-type structure with a flat roof. Inside wasn't much more. There were two rooms; the bedroom and the other room. The other room contained a small kitchen with an island made from polished stone, separating it from the entertainment area. The light blue walls absent of pictures and paintings. A small love seat and table and a couple swivel stools at the island made up the entirety of furniture in the other room. She'd never seen the bedroom.

The path there was filled with tiny bits of embedded metals and gems. It wasn't very well worn. She'd never noted that before, always coming with Gwond. She assumed it was his. Her mind a flutter with all the reasons she was upset with Hank, she didn't think as she flung the door to the cottage open.

A flash of teal light caught her eyes. She squinted, unsure what she'd seen. Chalking it up to nothing more than light from the blue ribbons in the sky shining through the windows, she glanced around. "Terina!"

Moving toward the center of the room, a faint scent hung in the air. She sniffed again but it was gone. "Terina!"

"In here. I need your help."

Terra pushed the bedroom door open to see a hand and a face peeking from under the bed. "What are you doing?"

"Get me out of here and I'll tell you everything."

Terra lifted the bed with a point of her finger. Terina rolled out from under it in troll form and pulled herself up. Dusting off her clothes, she marched toward Terra standing in the doorway.

"I demand to go home as me, now!" Fire blazed in her eyes and the freckles under them bounced as her face contorted.

"We have a deal. What did you learn?"

Terina brushed past her, their shoulders connecting, and continued her stride to the front door. Thrusting it open, she stepped outside.

Obviously she was upset, but why? What could possibly go wrong in a small cottage outside Rubina that no one knew about? Terra followed her outside. "What happened?"

Terina halted and spun on her heel, her troll plumage spreading out behind her back. "Can I tell you somewhere else? This place gives me the creeps."

Fine. She could do that, but where? Out of the seven realms, she chose Aradia. There was a part of her that felt most connected to it and safest there. It wasn't a rational feeling but was nonetheless where she took Terina, this time disguising her as an elf. She made her hair so long it brushed the ground, the tips of her ears poked out and her eyes took on a cerulean blue like the leaves of the trees.

In the Meradin woods she felt close to the mother she never knew and secluded from listening ears except for the trees. Clyde scampered away to find his chimu friends who he played with the time Rosette brought them to the forest. Terra stepped onto the porch of Rosette's cabin and motioned for Terina to join her.

Once Terina was settled on one of the porch chairs, she spilled her terrifying experience. "I wasn't alone. Someone else was there just before you. He was a troll, then a human. I didn't see his face because I dove under the bed. His legs and feet transformed before my eyes."

That didn't register in Terra's mind. Not many were able to transform, at least from troll to humanoid. Lycans shifted into wolves and some vampires into large cats, land fae into unicorns, sea fae into mer people, the dryad from tree to humanish, the elevarin of the darklands from insects and other creatures into humanoids… Maybe the list was longer than she thought and hybrids did have different capabilities. Her fae/elf friend, Cat, shifted into a catfish. "What else can you tell me?"

"He had blue sneakers."

That didn't tell her much, but she could see Terina was still tense as she tapped her fingers in her lap and kept moving her feet. For that moment she felt sympathy for the fae/warlock who tried to steal the Stones of Hovrath. "I can send you home, but I need to know everything."

Terina let out a deep, anxiety-filled breath and ran her sweaty palms along her pants. "Shadows swarmed from the corners and circled around him. They whispered and mumbled. I couldn't make out most of what they said as there were too many voices and I was scared, but your name came up more than once. That man. He leads the shadows I think. They are subservient to him."

The revelation sent shivers crawling like ants over Terra's skin. She'd seen the teal light but excused it as the sky shining through the window, smelled a male scent that dissipated quicker than she could pinpoint who it belonged.

It wasn't the first time she'd had a warning someone powerful was after her. Alex had warned her before she brought him to Provence. He was blind, but able to see things others couldn't. This wasn't the reason she'd sent Terina to Verboten but it made the threat more real. It was something she'd deal with. Getting back to their arrangement she asked, "What about the stones?"

"The trolls know nothing of them, but the shadows and their leader have the... exit stones."

10

The way Terra saw it, she had two potential next moves. She'd considered taking the enter stones and, with Hank, going to Marsidia, finding the source and ending this whole thing once and for all, but would such a rash move end it? There wouldn't be a way home without the exit stones, so if Marsidia and the warlocks proved to be unfriendly she wouldn't be able to return since the shadow things had the exit stones and she didn't have the steely heart to keep Terina in harm's way to find their location.

The exit stones didn't do the shadow things any good without the enter stones. This couldn't go on, neither would get further than they were. She needed to know more about the shadows called the Council of Divination.

She narrowed down her two choices; first she had a pure soul, one she thought many times might be Cyrus. It had a female voice but, if he was as strong as M'ra said, he could easily change his voice. In the antiquity room was a reverser. She couldn't pull a soul out from its glowing ball but Tania could and she knew where to find Tania. The idea of seeing her again excited her. It also forced her nerve endings to prickle, as they hadn't seen each other in months.

Would pulling the soul from its sphere answer any questions or raise more? If the soul was Cyrus, then that was solved. If it was someone else, maybe they could tell her more. The sphere radiated blue, meaning it was a soul with strong magic. She also considered the person whom Terina hid from. Could it be Cyrus? His soul was never harvested and his physical body never found. Was Cyrus an unharvested soul? Is that what the Council was?

If he was alive and well, as a strong realm walker he'd easily be able to change form as she did, but what would he be doing in Gwond's cottage in Verboten? That part didn't make sense and made her think there was a better explanation. Either way, she'd take the reverser and go to Tania.

The Ring of Betrayal

The other thing on her list excited her less and frightened her more. Alex was a seer of sorts. He'd warned her when she first met him that someone powerful was after her. She interpreted it to be M'ra at the time but that idea soon fizzled as M'ra warned her their battle was to come. She'd seen the future before her death. For months, she'd avoided thinking about it, closing her eyes and letting her body droop, she could no longer avoid what it was she and Hank were meant to accomplish.

She stared into Alex's fuzzy eyes as he ran a hand through his hair. "We can try again but I only see what it wants me to see."

That was fair. Terra pricked her arm. He needed DNA, and blood worked. It was also less painful than plucking a hair from her head. A dot of blood bubbled on her finger as she pressed it against Alex's. His head fell back and his eyes zoned out, then his body twitched. "There's a great light and a darkness in the shape of a double-headed monster. It has wings and horns and is wrestling with itself. That's it. That's all I see."

He blinked as his head dropped back into a normal upright position. She didn't know what that meant really. Wings and horns? Were they metaphorical? "It's what's after me?"

He nodded. "It has strong feelings for you; love and hate. You stand in its way of something."

Her tensions weren't eased but at least she knew more and had much to ponder. "That was a lot, Alex. Thank you."

Alex touched her arm. "Be careful."

It felt like the realms were closing in on her and everyone was turning against her except her friends. What was in Marsidia that everyone was after? Was it the source? If they destroyed it there'd be no magic and the realms would be destroyed. The fight over the Stones of Hovrath didn't make any sense.

Clyde bounced alongside her as she walked the circle of Provence, hanging in the woods. She stopped when she got to the geyser and sat, the grassy blades crunching under her butt. Deep in thought, she didn't hear the grass crunch when someone sat down beside her. Spoken words startled her into the present.

"I've been looking for you," Hank said as he sat on the ground beside her and stretched out his long legs. "I think we should send Terina back."

Studying his face, his dark eyes soft and sincere. Had she been too hard on him? He didn't mention the stones or his betrayal to her. "I already did. She's free to continue selling fairy dusted pastries to commoners." From Aradia she'd portalled her home, knowing she could find her again if she needed. Seeing how frightened and nervous she was, Terra didn't have the heart to forbid her. That would make her as vile as the fae or…the shadows. Was the monster with horns and wings wrestling with itself the shadows?

"Why so down?" he pressed.

Then something else came to mind. A way he could redeem himself. "If I send you to Lols, can you set up a meeting with the warlocks?"

His eye twitched. "That's dangerous. I can't have you in a situation like that. You sent them to Lols and locked them out. The only thing the warlocks want is passage home and you have that hidden."

"I know. That's why they won't harm me." She pet the blades of grass. "I need to know more about the situation. Why were they so desperate to get back after all these centuries?"

He pressed his hands over hers. It felt good and right in a time of massive brain confusion. She didn't pull away but it didn't mean forgiveness either. "I only know what I've told you, but seeing your power and how you awaken magic where it's dormant, I think it revived the desperation of my ancestors. I learned the ways of the warlock and how to harness power, but the day we kissed it awakened something else in me and I've been gaining new skills at a pace I've never witnessed, all related to you and the rune." Clyde pressed his nose along Hank's leg and when he went to pet him he scurried away then turned and stood on his back legs, wiggling his nose.

Everywhere she went, magic woke up so to speak. She was a conduit and channeler. She twisted her fingers in his. "You're saying they think what's down there can give them what I have?" But why were the shadows so desperate to get there?

His eyebrows formed a V. "I think what you have is special like no one else and I don't think they want what you have. They want what was stolen. You need to find the exit stones so we can go there ourselves." He paused. "I've been thinking. The vampire spies aren't likely to learn anything soon. It takes time to build trust. Send me to Lols as a bird. I can watch and listen without raising awareness or drawing attention."

It wasn't a bad idea. It was a brilliant idea.

11

Golden poppies swayed in the breeze as Terra looked at the special spot in the inbetween that she'd created. It was hers and only hers. The reverser in her backpack, Clyde on his harness, she turned around and marched to the tree, then reached in for the pure soul. Carefully, she rolled it into her backpack, mindful not to touch it with her hands.

Her next step was Hank. She was going to turn him into a bird, at least she hoped. Locks weren't a challenge for her anymore as she unlocked the door at Provence Academy that led to the curtain between Provence City and Lols. Energy bounced through her like a heartbeat when she crossed the curtain. Its beat parallel to the rhythmic energy that was a part of her. Energy was different in all realms, some softer, some more effervescent. All but one beat in unison with the energy in her. Navarin. Its energy worked contrary to the smooth beat that pumped inside her.

The huge, boring room spread out before them. It lacked any décor and was there simply as a curtain between the realms. They followed the steps leading down to the door that would place them outside the twin academy in Virginia. Mountains as far as the eye could see spread out as the sun and its golden rays rose above their tops.

The spring morning air fresh with a touch of moisture. Green plants bloomed in pinks and violets. The vines climbing the walls of the empty twin academy bloomed in blues and whites. Lols was always a comfort to her, but something felt different, more alive. She couldn't pinpoint it.

She didn't need the elevators anymore but liked them. No matter where in Lols she was, an elevator was near and would take her anywhere in Lols she asked. They stepped into the swirling energy of color and out into the quintessential Canadian town where Hank had lived and worked with the warlocks. It reminded her of how she and Hank met, trapped in an elevator.

He'd been a steady part of her life since and she was finding it difficult to stay upset with him. Had he betrayed her? Would she have done the same thing if their roles were reversed? Why was her life so hard?

Turning to Hank, she studied him, his braids falling over his shoulders, resting on his firm chest. "What type of bird should I make you?"

"A robin. They are the most common and won't draw attention."

She thought about that. Forming the image of the popular, red-breasted bird in her mind. She closed her eyes and concentrated as she imagined Hank as that bird. When she opened her eyes, Hank was gone. Fluttering in the air was a robin with braids, tiny braids. Crap! She focused on them as the bird flew to a tree branch and perched.

How do you feel? she asked through their telepathic connection.

I don't know, how does a bird feel? was his sharp, sarcastic response.

She concentrated on his form, attempting to get rid of the braids. They changed into long feathers. She sighed, it would have to do. *I'll meet you here in two days.*

He shook his head and flew away, a bit lopsided at first then he straightened himself out.

Now she had to get to Tania. She was a student at NYU and lived in Greenwich

Village. It was early. They'd snuck up the stairs before anyone at the school stirred. She'd miss classes. The dean might call Rosette. She could go to her classes then return to Lols. No, Rosette wasn't the mean, purse-lipped, uptight elf she'd thought at first. She told her the truth about her parents, helped her get to Drakonia during the lockdown where she could get M'ra's help.

Stepping into another elevator, she pictured Tania's brownstone. When the swirls of color vanished, she was standing on the sidewalk outside it. Suddenly she felt awkward. It had been months since she'd seen her. She dragged her feet as she climbed the couple steps to Tania's door and sucked in a deep breath.

Swallowing her nerves, she knocked. A few moments later the door opened a sliver. Tania's face filled the space between the door and frame. Her golden-brown eyes the first thing Terra took in. Terra's eyes drifted to the delicate gold nose ring and the snake ring tattoo on her upper arm as she held it against the door frame. Her dark hair shorter. Last time she saw her it was shaved on one side and hung to her shoulders on the other. Now it was above her ears, short on the sides. Clyde sniffed at her, standing on his back legs. "Come in. I wasn't expecting you."

That wasn't quite the welcome Terra was hoping for. Shaking it off, she took in the tiny studio apartment. It looked the same as when Terra visited last. The burgundy loveseat faced the bay window. The colorful character of the street and other homes a picturesque view. The bamboo dressing screen between the room and bed closed. "I'm sorry I didn't contact you first."

"It's no problem. If you're here, you need me."

Was that all? Is that how she thought of her? "No. I mean yes, but that's not the only reason."

Tania smiled as she took a seat on a stool at the slender bar. "It's OK. You don't need to apologize."

Her words were reassuring but Terra felt horribly out of place. The feelings she'd felt for her overwhelmed her, yet they were much less than what she felt for Hank. Was that part of what she was holding on to? Part of the reason she wouldn't commit more to Hank? Even the excuse she found for seeing her today?

She sat on the barstool next to Tania. A crunch filled her ears and she glanced to the side to see the bamboo dressing screen pulled back and a beautiful young woman padding towards them. A pink T-shirt hung over her healthy sized chest, nothing hidden as she lacked a bra. Cream-colored shorts peaked out from under the oversized shirt.

Terra stumbled nervously over her words, "I'm sorry… I didn't… I should go." She jumped off the stool.

"Silly, I'm going to make coffee you should stay and have a cup," the woman said.

Terra's gaze moving from the sex-in-a-pristine-package woman to Tania. Her expression didn't read 'get out of my house' yet Terra wanted nothing more than to run away. Of course, she'd moved on so had Terra…sort of. "No, I'll come back when you don't have company." It was the white elephant moment she hoped she'd never have to face. A part of her was glad Tania had found someone, another part of her was jealous it wasn't her, and another part of her yearned even more for Hank.

Tania reached for the woman's hands. "I'll meet you later."

The woman leaned toward Tania and kissed her. Terra dropped her eyes, feeling like she was eavesdropping on something she shouldn't.

On Tania's insistence, Terra stayed, taking a seat on the sofa. The woman went behind the dressing screen and returned. Terra didn't turn around to watch but listened as her footfalls stopped near the bar, more kissing she was sure, then started again moving past the sofa toward the door. She didn't stop or look back as she stepped out, closing the door behind her.

Terra stood, facing Tania. "I'm so sorry. I hope I haven't caused any problems."

"You haven't. It feels weird having you and her here at the same time though, but we had something that couldn't survive the long distance. What Sharae and I have is new. She likes ghosts. We have that in common. It's what brought us together. I haven't... told her yet, though, about my abilities."

There it was. That singular moment that cemented their bond as friends. They'd been through something amazing and scary together and, against the odds, succeeded. A sudden swell of happiness pushed into her chest, followed by relief. "I've met someone too but it's more complicated."

"Do you want to talk about it?"

She wanted desperately to talk about it, but didn't know where to begin and felt uncomfortable telling a woman who she'd had feelings for about her new...whatever Hank was. "Let's just leave it at complicated. My life has been nothing but complications since my father died. Hank, that's his name, offers more complications, ones I don't even understand."

"Let me get some clothes on and we'll talk," Tania said as she stood.

For the first time since Terra arrived, she glanced at the tight green tank top covering Tania and the bikini panties not covering much. The curves of her full behind barely covered by the thin underwear. She was hot! Putting her dramatic teenage hormones in check, she waited until Tania reemerged from behind the screen in a pair of loose jeans with holes in the knees. The green tank top traded for a blue T-shirt with the name of a bar or restaurant on it.

They got down to business and Terra told her about the shadows and the imminent danger she felt, then pulled the pickaxe reverser out of her backpack.

Handing it to Tania, her eyes widened as she took it. Its pearly handle shone in the sun spreading through the curtain. She ran a hand along the wooden head. "What does this do?"

"It pulls souls out of their spheres." It wasn't like she actually knew, but Gwond had always been honest with her, sometimes to a fault, even though all his truths had deeper implications. His knowledge took her on many a journey, yet she didn't trust him completely. He was an adult, a teacher.

"I've never heard of such a thing." She lifted it into the air. "It's light." She turned her eyes away from the pickaxe and met Terra's. "What am I using it for?" The new toy wore off quick as Tania understood it meant she was expected to use it, trepidation filling her words.

Terra's backpack resting against her chest, she opened it wide exposing the pure soul. Tania's gaze dropped into the backpack and a gasp escaped her mouth. "How did you… get that?"

"Well," Terra began, not choosing to find the right words but to spill. "Clyde found it when I was sent to Thraves. There was a human vampire the vampires in Drakonia collected and I was forced to Thraves to help save the girl. The minister thought my blood would do the trick. I didn't understand how, but Clyde's life was in the balance, so I did it." She didn't stop there but filled her in on how she was a realm walker, what a realm walker was, the invasion of the realms, and how she and Hank expelled them, bringing her to the current moment. "The soul speaks to me and I think it can help me."

Tania didn't hide how overwhelmed she was. Terra could nearly see her head spinning. She opened her mouth but words didn't come out at first. "Wh… I… It's pure and should be sent to Tranquility. I harvest, not unharvest. There's no way of knowing if the soul will be irreparably damaged."

She was right, undeniably, yet Terra had a feeling no harm would come to the soul. "It talks to me, guides me when it wants, other times it's very quiet like right now."

Tania scratched her head in thought. "I can't do this without talking with my instructor. Go behind the room divider. I'll have him come back in spirit. It can't be tracked."

No! She wanted to scream not to bring anyone else into this, but didn't. Tania was new to harvesting, her skills different than harvesters in Thraves, as she could harvest souls in her physical form not having to cross the veil into Lols. Terra sat on her bed, the bamboo divider between them, and listened as she asked him to return in spirit form, asserting she needed his help.

Tania pulled the bamboo back. "You can come out now."

Within moments, a tall man with a goatee materialized in his spirit form. His hand tugging at the wiry hair falling from his chin. Terra recognized him. He was the harvester, Metford, who was voted off the tribunal for the debacle with Tania. Instead of going to the tribunal, which he should have as a diplomat, he listened to Bane. She'd gained some respect for Bane since then, but still didn't really trust him. Together, they kept Tania a secret. Her soul was meant to be harvested the day she fell into Blood River, but wasn't, and they had a use for her as a hybrid harvester.

Terra pulled her lips back as she almost spoke without thinking. Tania was his punishment. The words stayed in her head.

Metford stared at both girls with an expression showing he didn't agree with whatever they were planning, even before he knew what it was. Terra explained how she found the soul and how it spoke to her. He stared at her, tugging at his chestnut-colored goatee. She continued and explained the reverser.

'Where did you get that?' That's what he said, not 'You found a pure soul rummaging around Traves?', 'Hey we've been looking for that', or 'Cool a reverser' or even 'We wondered where that went'. "Can you help, or do I need to try this on my own?"

That got his attention, and he cleared his throat. She knew he didn't always play by the rules. If he did, he'd still be on the tribunal instead of here now. "Against my better judgement," he said after a long pause. "In order to reverse harvest you must place the stones in the reverse and use the special pickaxe to pull the soul out."

Terra watched as Tania laid the soul in the middle of the room and placed the rocks she brought with her to Lols from the realms around it. Carefully, she picked up the reverser and brought it over the circle.

Metford guided her as she lowered the axe head. She kept it steady above the sphere, as if having second thoughts, then brought it down gently and touched the sphere with the tip.

"Pull slow, you don't want to damage it."

She took a deep breath and, with a steady hand, pulled upwards. The violet sphere elongated and started to take shape. Tania swallowed and Terra felt her nerves, pressing a hand to her shoulder to show her she was with her. Once the soul was drawn out, a translucent woman stood between the rocks. The soul's translucent hair shimmered in many colors. She knew what the woman was and it certainly wasn't Cyrus. She sighed a bit of relief, yet she'd hoped maybe it was. That meant the possibility of Cyrus being alive still existed. She couldn't close the book on that possibility.

"You're a realm walker," Terra said as she moved to the side of Tania.

The soul's lips curved and she swore if she could cry as a soul she was doing so. "Terra, you've grown up so beautiful."

Shivers ran across Terra's skin as things clicked into place. She knew this woman, felt her energy inside of her. It was tingly and filled with love that radiated outward and filled the entire room. "Mom?"

12

She felt as if they had a lifetime to catch up on, but there wasn't time and all the words she planned to say and ask the soul escaped her mind.

Her mother's soothing voice that'd carried her through so much since she'd found the sphere spoke, "You know who you are, what I was and, for you to be here, having the ability to pull me from the sphere then your father." Her translucent eyes looked deep into Terra's. "He risked everything for you and he loved you."

There was never a moment when she hadn't felt her father's love or questioned it. What she'd missed all her life was having a mother. Terra wanted to step into the circle and put her arms around her. All her life, she'd dreamed of meeting her, dreamed of a life with her in it. Finally, here they were, and she couldn't do any of the things she dreamt of. Another thought crested her mind. When her mother referred to her father did she mean the one who raised her or the one whose DNA she carried. "Which father?"

Thorns poked her heart that she even asked the question. Her mother's face stayed gentle and soft as her colorful eyes stayed on Terra's and carried the *you know* glance. "The father who raised you. Cyrus was a moment. He's not important."

The bite in her words stung Terra. She understood their meaning. Cyrus hurt her, used her, maybe. Enough about her fathers. "Mom," Terra swallowed, "shadows, they're after me. I have something they want."

Her soft, translucent eyes grew dark. "I don't know anything of shadows but I would guess you're in the company of those who might. There is something I need you to do, something important. We don't have much time, I feel the pull. Can you do this?"

What now! Terra's mind screamed, not at her mom but the weight on her shoulders just got so heavy she felt them plummet to the floor. Terra nodded, not knowing what she was about to ask of her.

"First, you must know it's not your actions but actions of another. Don't blame yourself."

There it was, guilt squished her guts into a tight ball. All she wanted was to feel her mother's arms around her but it couldn't be. She had to be a realm walker, child of realm walkers, with infinite duties related to realm walking and peace.

She held out her hands as if Terra could touch them. "Serenity Tree. It's been shrinking. It was so large and beautiful with its golden-tipped leaves and shiny fruit. It was the whole center of Aradia and majestic. It's shrunk so much. We found scrolls and paintings of the tree. It grew from desolation and destruction. Elves didn't notice it getting smaller, time was forgotten. I was about your age when I started taking measurements. Each year its base is smaller."

Terra was more confused than ever. "I don't understand."

"You must save the tree. When Serenity Tree perishes, so will life. You are the reason the realms stand at all and they may continue, but life will perish. The tree isn't nurtured by life alone but something more — magic."

Terra's head felt like a two-year-old's drawing, with squiggles of colors and lines that didn't connect. "Is that the real reason for the cleansing?" she asked, trying to piece anything together.

"No, I don't know. Your biological father, Cyrus, he was a bad boy. The sexy guy you know isn't good for you, but you do it anyways. When I found out I was pregnant with you I told him and he broke my heart. But that's what I needed to see the one who was always there. We escaped to Lols to save you and I went back. Times were bad. Your father begged me not to leave. I didn't have a choice. I had to save you and the tree. Cyrus, he pushed me to give up your location but I wouldn't. I didn't trust him…"

Like a CD with a scratch, her mind stuck on one thing. "I don't understand."

Her beautiful face emitted the familiar, parently *you will* expression. "My tiara. It carries a seed from the tree. That seed is the key. My time is nearing an end." Her form faded and brightened.

"Mom, no. I don't know what to do." Terra broke down and pressed her head in her hands.

"Yes, you do. The answers are in you. I love you."

Terra lifted her head from her hands, tears on her cheeks, her nose burning as tears streamed uncontrollably. Her mother faded, her form coiled into a blinking sphere. She'd always wanted her mother and the moment in her life that she finally met her was filled with the horrible destiny of being a realm walker. She loathed what she was as her pink carnation tattoo burned into her skin with phantom pains.

"I love you, Mom." A blubbery mess of tears and snot, Terra watched her mother's soul sphere vanish. Dropping to her knees, a surge of energy filling her, she reached a hand into the circle, but it was too late.

Tania dropped next to her and wrapped her arm around Terra as she cried into her hands.

It was Metford who broke the silence as he wiped the tears under his own eyes, moved by the encounter. "I don't expect you trust me, and for good reason, but she's right, Terra. You are incredible. You must use that to save the tree. What she says is true, if the tree withers so does life, so the shadows chasing you and anything else happening in your life or ours isn't important unless you save it."

His words, although not comforting, helped her put something into perspective. The shadows she may never find but the tree… she knew exactly where to find it and how to communicate with it. There was more than a grain of truth to her mother's words.

"I knew your father," Metford admitted, unable to look her in the eye.

Of course he knew him. Cyrus was the realm walker of Thraves. Her expectant gaze met his almost guilty one.

"He wasn't always bad, but was never exactly good. A part of him rebelled against life. There was a darkness in him and a hunger for power. His soul's never been found and is probably buried, waiting for something like that reverser. Keep it safe." With those words, his spirit form vanished.

His words pressed on Terra's heart as more a warning about her father than anything. Cyrus wasn't her concern, dead or alive. The tree and her mother's words forced her mind back to the fae dungeon and the drawings, then flipped to the tiara. The one her father gave her their last Christmas together. He said it was her mom's. In the center was a golden stone. It was the seed from the tree. If all life perished, the seed could be planted. No, she said it was the key, but the key to what?

Tania helped her up and offered her a glass of water and a tissue. It was the two of them. As challenging as it was, she had to stay focused. "Do you…know about the …shadows?"

Tania sat a glass of ice water on the bar. "There are some things you should know. I planned on telling you, but you side-tracked me with the pure soul." She took a pause then came around and sat on the bar stool beside Terra.

It took her a moment, as if trying to figure out how to approach what she needed to say. "A few months ago, there were reports of people falling from the sky, others who showed up in places they'd never been without memories of how they got there. That was you. You sent them here and it caused a movement. More than that, people are finding magic, learning they can do things. There's a hashtag going around social media #awakening. You'll find stories from those who lost their memories, the ones who survived their drop from the sky, and ordinary people who can suddenly access magic. I feel the energy in the air, everything is brighter and more alive than it ever has been."

That was a lot for Terra to unpack. When she sent the warlocks, vampires, and werewolves back to Lols she had never thought they went blasting out of Drakonia and literally fell in Lols. She hadn't thought they'd face any adverse effects, such as losing their memories. That wasn't part of what she was trying to do. M'ra had crumbled into a pile of dust and she was lost, saddened. She'd let that anger fuel her as she let the energy build then explode. Was it that emotion that made the explosion of energy more intense, that forced them to forget? Was she putting too much on herself? She wasn't alone. Hank played a part. Had he used one of his runes to make them forget? "Show me."

Tania reached over and plucked her cell phone from the kitchen side of the bar. In a moment she handed her the phone. Terra scrolled through, story after story of people and magic they were suddenly capable of, from spell casting to telekinesis. The stories changed as she scrolled further to others who told their story of how they forgot pieces of their life. Sure, most people wouldn't take any of it seriously and the government would treat it like aliens, but from what she read the movement was gaining strength and momentum.

"You and Hank awoke something in Lols. There's something remarkable between the two of you and I think you should embrace it." Tania wrapped an arm over Terra's shoulder and met her gaze, her eyes searching Terra's. "I think maybe whatever you woke up could have something to do with the shadows you speak of."

13

It had been months since Terra got the group together, but she needed them now. Whatever was happening was more than one person alone could solve. There were too many random moving pieces that she understood on a personal level fit together, but they didn't fit. She needed help.

Unable to sit still, she paced. During the invasion, when refugees from all realms escaped to Provence City, the portable had been in use. Dry dishes hung in the drainer by the sink. Towels were folded neatly in the bath. There were signs everywhere that the place hadn't been vacant for long.

REALM WALKER

When Kinzo first brought her to the portable with Tania as a safe place she could hide out, the place was dusty and carried a stale odor. After Tania went home, they continued to use the place to meet up and plot. That's what she needed now. Friends.

Kayln, her short lavender hair tied up in two ponytails on top of her head, bounced through the door. Her effervescent fae attitude slighted by the mournful looks of Nalysse who trailed behind her. Since she and Kinzo had their falling out she'd changed, but not in a bad way. She was more… Terra couldn't put a finger on the word, but different. Her tops and jeans tighter, she was more aloof. It was a bad girl look and not a horrible one on her.

Hyacinth and Caspen entered next. Instead of directly joining Kayln and Nalysse, Hyacinth folded her arms around Terra as if she read all the insanity going on in her mind. Hyacinth wasn't a mind wiping or bending vampire. She was a shifter. Caspen slipped past them and joined the others at the table. Some people might think a vampire and an elf would never last, but they made a great couple and were as strong as ever.

Kinzo entered next. A tank, long shorts, and flip flops, he looked like a surfer minus the sun-kissed blonde hair. His elfin, uncut hair was tied in the same braided style he'd worn for months. He didn't completely ignore Nalysse but didn't sit next to her either. She hoped whatever was happening between them wouldn't affect their ability to help.

Last, Meesha entered. Her tall, lanky, muscled frame shadowed the room from the door as the fake sun in Provence was beginning to set. Lycans didn't have to work to keep their physique. It was a gift of the subspecies.

Terra stood as she was the one who was to speak. She'd called everyone there. The candle they always had on the table was moved during the lockdown and placed in a drawer. She'd found it and taken it out. When the words left her mouth, they sounded like the ramblings of a lost kid. "The inner realm of Marsidia, where the warlocks are from, has the source of magic. I'm an amplifier of that magic. The veils and curtains were created when realm walkers were created. Then there's the Serenity Tree. It's shrinking. A little every year. One day it will be gone and a seed is in my tiara to do something…" she paused and caught her breath, "and shadows want me dead."

Nalysse raised a brow. "The Serenity Tree is life. That's what elves are taught. It connects all the realms just like the river." Her words succinct, yet answering nothing.

Meesha tapped the table for a minute. "OK, you're saying these things are related?"

"I don't know, maybe. In some way, yes."

Kinzo, with his deep in thought, somber expression said, "There's no past that includes Marsidia. How do we know it exists?"

That was easy, or was it? *Did it exist?* Was she chasing the shadows? She had the Stones of Hovrath, but couldn't read them. Regardless, the warlocks and shadows were searching for the stones, therefore they were important and, even though she couldn't see Marsidia, she believed it existed. "The warlocks. They've carried the stories verbally for centuries and I've seen the Stones of Hovrath. They caused the disturbance in Navarin."

Kayln, the only fae in the room, seconded Terra: "The disturbance was always said to be a direct connection to the tree. By taking the stones, the disturbance is gone, the connection is lost, and the waters are calm."

The elves exchanged glances. "Do you have proof the tree is shrinking? Because that's a dangerous accusation," Kinzo stated with a curious eye.

"Yes." She omitted the part about her mom. It was too painful yet, but this was something she had to do and she'd found proof. "The tree's been shrinking since before the stones were taken." She unfurled tapestries she'd borrowed from the antiquities room. "Don't ask. During the invasion Hank and I were taken below the palace in Navarin to a lower dungeon." From the corner of Terra's eye she caught Kayln's pouty lips. "There were pictures on the wall. One was the Serenity Tree. It was massive, taking up almost an entire wall. If you study the scrolls and dates you can see how it gets smaller."

"Those are tapestries, not actual pictures," Kayln said with a roll of her eyes, dismissing the tree and its importance.

Caspen, who was never one to jump in unless he was sure or had evidence, said, "If we accept these pictures as true replicas, everything else in them is correct, then we also accept the Serenity Tree and the river are life's connection to each other. Trees need water. The veils and curtains have sealed realms not because they needed to be sealed but because our ancestors couldn't get along. They built barriers to keep the peace. If we accept everything else as true then we accept the warlock stories as true. Marsidia exists and so does the source of magic. Trees don't grow from water alone, they need soil and sunshine. In this case, the source of magic. If everything is sealed, the tree can't grow. Magic and life will fade."

All eyes looked at the quiet genius who responded in simplified terms, "You need to get to the source to save the tree and life."

Yes! This is exactly what Terra needed. She threw her arms around him. "Your brain is magic!"

Hyacinth put a kink in it: "How does Terra fit into this and what about the cleansing?" Since it was revealed Terra was a realm walker, the cleansing couldn't be kept quiet. People talked as if they were free of a heavy burden on their shoulders. Terra guessed they were.

"Wouldn't their magic return to the source?" Hyacinth asked.

"My devil's advocate," Caspen replied. "Realm walkers are the source, or walking pieces of it anyways. That's why Terra amplifies it. The spell used level 4 magic and sacrifice. It attached realm walkers directly to the source. Their magic may have returned to it or it may have accumulated in the only living realm walker." Caspen's eyes flashed to Terra. "We don't know, but Terra must see what the source wants, what it needs, and we're going to help her."

Terra swallowed. "There's something standing in the way. Once I go, I can't return. I don't have the exit stones."

Kinzo squared his shoulders. "Where did you get the maps?"

"A secret place filled with all kinds of old stuff."

"Does any of that old stuff offer a way to Marsidia? There's usually more than one way to solve a problem and there's always more than one way to travel into realms, especially when they are blocked off." Kinzo's words ended in silence. Each teen looked at him then Terra.

She remembered her mom's tiara had a seed from the Serenity Tree that she'd said was a key. Maybe it was a key to a device that could take her to Marsidia and return her. It would be obvious if they all went down to the antiquity room, but there was a lot of stuff. It would take her too long to find it on her own if it was there. "Tonight. I'll take three of you with me."

14

Meesha was the tallest and there were high shelves in the antiquity room, Kayln was the only one who could read Old Fae, and Caspen was the genius, so those were the three she chose. On the way down she explained not to touch anything as everything was a type of magical device. Her eyes automatically glanced at Kayln.

"I'm capable of not touching things," Kayln harrumphed, but Terra wasn't so sure. She had the bounciness and innocence of a four-year-old at times.

When the floor landed Kayln gasped, "Where did all this stuff come from?"

The Ring of Betrayal

"The realm walkers collected them and brought them here where they'd be safe." It wasn't unlike what she'd done with the enter Stones of Hovrath, Merla's Realm Grimoire with the spell that made realm walkers, and the pure soul that turned out to be her mother.

Thinking about it she was like a ferret. Collecting and hiding things. Terra unzipped her backpack and pulled out the tiara. "We're looking for something this will fit into."

"That's elf." Caspen held out his hand, "Do you mind?"

Terra handed it to him. He held it steady in his palm then tilted his head at various angles. "Where did you get this?"

"It was my mom's. My father gave it to me the last Christmas we had together."

"It's definitely elf. Handcrafted and quite valuable."

Terra's mother, the Aradian realm walker, was given a valuable gift. "In the center is a seed from the Serenity Tree. It unlocks whatever it is we are searching for."

A smile grew on Caspen's face. He held the tiara up to his eyes and studied the golden seed. "That's clever."

The four searched high and low. There was an overwhelming amount of stuff in the room but nothing that would fit the seed or looked like it would.

"Bring the tiara," Meesha said, as she stood beside Caspen who knelt to eye level with the table, his eyes studying the object on it. Terra handed it to him and he laid it on the table next to a thing that looked like gears.

Of course! Now Terra remembered. When Gwond brought her here she'd noted the artifact. It wasn't anything special and looked like a gear from an old-fashioned pocket watch. It was bigger, but also had an oval spot empty of something. With the tiara facing it on the table, it was clear the seed would fit inside the oval. Gwond called it an ascendant and said something about it being used to travel to Lols. What she hadn't asked is why someone would go to Lols. No, it wasn't used for that. It was created to travel to other realms, and maybe even Marsidia, but without the seed as a key it was useless.

"We saw the plans for this in Lols." Meesha stared at Terra who blinked without recollection. "The teacher with all the stuff. She has a book in her office. You took pictures on your phone."

Vaguely, Terra remembered it. So much happened that day. When touching the exit Stones of Hovrath, that she had no idea at the time what they were except something that buzzed energy on contact. The crack in the Verboten veil and the crown of the dead king Kayln found, along with the spooky skull Nalysse found.

The Ring of Betrayal

Kayln bubbled as she talked and Terra ran through their adventure in Lols in her head. "It fits like a puzzle piece." She met the table at eye level across from Caspen.

"There's writing on it," Meesha noted. Her predator vision was acute.

Kayln stood. "What does it say?"

"I can't read it but I think you could if there was more light and maybe a magnifying glass."

Terra collected the ascendant in a small bag she'd brought. Putting it and the tiara into her backpack, they headed upstairs. They'd look at it tomorrow after classes.

Skipping class again, Terra returned to Lols. She couldn't leave Hank there indefinitely as a robin. In order to not be recognized, in case the warlocks were lurking about, she transformed herself into a blonde, middle-aged woman and Clyde into a poodle. *Hank,* she called with her mind as she strolled the main street of the tiny town.

She knew he was here. She felt his energy and the invisible magic cord connecting them. *Where are you?* She stopped for a coffee and sat at one of the tables under a green umbrella. She figured if she kept moving it would take him longer to catch up to her. A few sips into the coffee, a bird landed on the back frame of the chair next to her. The long feathers on its head gave away that it was Hank. *There you are.*

She stood and strolled toward the elevator that would take them back to the twin academy then home to Provence. First, she needed to transform him back to himself, but not around others. He flew along behind her as she turned the corner into the alley and stopped. He landed on the ground next to her and she commanded him to return to his normal physical form.

In seconds, he stood in front of her. They fast walked to the elevator. "Lols is filled with waking magic like a flower blooming. The wizard isn't upset, well, a little. I got close enough to listen. This new enchanted world humans live in is opening opportunities for warlocks." Hank's face bubbled in the effervescence she expected from Kayln.

That was great, but she had more pressing matters and the new awakened world wouldn't exist for long unless she fixed it. "We may have a way to get back from Marsidia," she stated in a cool, calm tone as they stepped into the elevator.

Within moments, they exited the elevator and entered the twin academy. In the couple days since he'd been a bird his facial hair had grown, giving him a sexy but rough appearance. He closed his thumb and pointer finger around his scruffy chin. "You found the exit stones?"

"No, something else."

The Ring of Betrayal

As they climbed the stairs they talked and she explained the ascendant and the Serenity Tree. He'd never heard of an ascendant. In the hallway on the third floor, outside the door to Provence, she stopped.

Seeing Tania and meeting her mother, she realized moments may be fleeting but they stay with the soul forever. Tania was a moment, a beautiful moment, but Hank was something more, even Tania realized that. She'd been hard on him. He didn't deserve the way she treated him. It was a barrier she'd built to protect herself after her father's death and all she'd been through since. She wanted to trust people, but didn't trust him. He was too close and whatever was between them was too powerful.

How could she blame him for building his own barrier? Her having the stones and him the ability to read the spell was a fair trade. Neither of them could go to Marsidia without the other. She faced him and glanced into his dark eyes. "I'm sorry. You're right. If Marsidia protects the source of all magic in every realm it's not a place people should travel to carelessly. You having the ability to read the spell and me having the stones keeps it safe from others. If the Serenity Tree is truly dying then that is a noble enough reason to travel to Marsidia and face the source. I want you by my side."

He folded his arms over her back and pulled her to his chest. She closed her eyes and embraced the moment. Her mind saw him pushing her against the wall and pressing his lips to hers in a hunger matching her own. Desire screamed inside her and wanton urges. No, it wasn't time. She fought with all her strength to not give in. "What do you mean Serenity Tree is dying?"

15

Terra swallowed her pride and went to Rosette. Not because she wanted her advice, but because she'd skipped class a lot and knew she owed her an explanation. While she was having dinner with her not real aunt, her friends were scouring the library, and Hank and Kayln were reading the scrolls from the Antiquity room for how to use the ascendant. Unfortunately, her pictures were of the drawing, not the words accompanying it on how the ascendant worked. The writing on it was merely a spell, not directions. Could it only be used from certain locations, at specific times of year, or days of the week?

Realm Walker

After she explained everything to Hank, he comforted her and vowed to do all he could to help. Their moment together fresh on her mind. *Why was she so stubborn?* She felt his firm body next to hers, relished it, empathized with him, yet she couldn't do the one thing she felt inside she needed to do. Her pig-headedness wouldn't allow it.

Rosette wasn't much of a cook, but she did cater to Terra's commoner food, so they ate different things. Rosette had some type of eggplant-looking thing but it was orange and Terra had a microwave chicken and rice dinner from the freezer. Not having more details, and not sure how she'd take it, Terra didn't mention going to Marsidia. She merely made excuses for her absences.

Rosette's tiny lips bunched together in frustration, but her words were calm. "A realm walker has a large burden to carry. You must keep peace within the realms, but you also need to graduate. I've spoken with the dean who is willing to let your absences this week slide so long as they don't happen again."

Ugh! Two months from graduation and she might have to miss and be a high school dropout. Definitely a good choice not to mention it to Rosette. "About that." Terra pushed the chicken into the rice. "Do you know anything about shadow people?"

Rosette's brows lowered and her blue eyes narrowed. "What do you know?"

You can't follow up a question with a question! She narrowed her eyes at Rosette and stared hard.

Rosette's pursed lips opened and she gave in first, her eyes shifting toward the window above the sink. "The Council of Divination. It's a myth. When things went bad, people blamed shadow creatures, calling them the Council of Divination. It doesn't exist."

Sure it didn't. Terra had learned everything existed. As a kid growing up in Lols, there were stories of all the subspecies in the realms; fairies, elves, trolls, shifters, vampires. Of course, this was no different. A myth containing at least some truth. "Where do these come from?"

Shifting her gaze to Terra, Rosette studied her face. Terra held her curious teenage expression and chewed to avoid the possibility Rosette might see through her act. "Unharvested dark souls."

Yup! They were real. She wasn't skipping any further down that trail and did a conversation one-eighty. "Tell me about the Serenity Tree."

Rosette lowered a spoonful of eggplant thing from her lips. "We've discussed it before."

"I know but…who takes care of it?"

Rosette's tiny lips spread into a smile. "The elves, of course." She shoved the bite in her mouth.

"There's not like a group or person who takes care of it?"

After Rosette swallowed the bite she explained, "Your mom had a special relationship with the Serenity Tree but it is the job of all elves, not a singular group." Terra noted the tension in her words. She was definitely holding something back and unwilling to tell her more.

They discussed the awakening happening in Lols. Rosette didn't seem overly shocked about it and how the five Terra brought back from Lols would soon be ready to take their places as diplomats. In a time when commoners were coming around it seemed perfect for them to take their places on the tribunal.

All of them had been making great progress learning to control magic. Alex was focusing the visions better and Mario was shifting with ease thanks to Meesha.

When Terra parted, she went straight to the portable. Clyde instinctively, or through the psychic connection Terra believed they shared, ran ahead of her and waited outside the portable door. When she reached it, she opened it and he scampered inside.

Kayln and Hank pored over the scrolls. Warlock and old fae were similar languages, so both could read them. They were also her only two friends who could, with the exception of Halsey and Bjorn, but Halsey being the Diama wasn't safe to bring in on this one, especially if the fae were somehow responsible for the fall of the realms, or whatever was happening. Bjorn might let something slip in a weak moment when his tongue was buried in Halsey's mouth. Terra couldn't be sure anymore.

"Anything yet?" Terra asked as she reached the table.

Kayln lifted her head and blew out a frustrated breath. "Maybe." She pointed to words on the page and a picture of something that looked like the ascendant, but it was larger. "It's blurred. Neither of us can make out the words!"

All Terra saw were fuzzy squiggles of lines. "Could it be a spell or could a spell unblur it?"

Kayln and Hank met gazes as if they were perplexed neither of them had thought of that. Their ah ha moment was interrupted when the door swung open. Caspen entered, breathless, like he'd run the entire way.

"I found something!" He pressed his comicay and a page of text appeared in the air from his memories. "According to this, the tree was fullest when life was anew. The fact that anew is used instead of new I think is important. Anew would mean life is cyclic.

New would mean fresh, never born before. 'The tree is fullest' also suggests the tree is expected to shrink over time."

In his excitement, Caspen continued, pointing in the air to another set of passages. "The tree's liveliness depends on the health of life. Any strife between subspecies and realms will make it shrink at a faster rate," he said, interpreting the text.

That struck a bell in Terra's mind. In her mom's life, hate and fear filled the hearts and minds of the subspecies towards the realm walkers.

Caspen pointed to another passage. "Its roots spread through every realm and dangle in the inner realm of Marsay."

"Marsidia! Sometimes it's called Marsay," Hank noted, bubbling life champagne. Caspen glanced toward him and nodded, as he'd already figured that out.

Studying their faces Caspen said one more thing: "I think the tribunal knows all this."

"How?" Terra asked.

"Hyacinth may have overheard some of the members talking when she met Devan for lunch yesterday after their weekly meeting." Devan was Hyacinth's brother and the youngest diplomat on the tribunal.

A bell chimed again in Terra's head. That's what Rosette kept from her when she asked about the tree. All the pieces started to shift into place and she remembered the conversation she had with the silver-leafed Fryca during her last plant connections class. It told her *they* were always with her. Implying the trees and life. But who was with the Serenity Tree that had been taken for granted so much that it had shrunk terribly over the years?

Marya had taken fruit from the tree, describing it and drawing it in her journal. Its base so wide, its roots spread through the waters. Its roots now visible as the waters were lower. Its trunk still huge, but it lacked new growth on its branches. "We need to go to the tree now!" Terra insisted.

"We should get Nalysse and Kinzo. It may take all of us to speak with the tree," Caspen said.

Terra glanced to Hank, who gave her a knowing nod. It wasn't only that she was a walking, breathing, sentient slice of the source but, Nalysse and Kinzo had strife between them and that wouldn't help connect with the tree. In fact, it might harm the tree more if the words were true that strife between the subspecies would make it shrink faster. They couldn't take the chance. "No! We do this alone."

16

It was just as Marya described it. The Serenity Tree's large branches extended beyond the moat of water surrounding it. A few silver leaves floated on the glassy water, stuck between its thick roots that jutted out from the surface. Terra glanced into the water and felt as if she could fall into it.

The tree trunk was thick and erect. The dirt surrounding the moat, cut in layers, displayed how much the tree had shrunk over the years. In Marya's journal, she described it as if there wasn't a way to get to the center of the moat and touch the tree. Looking at it now, Terra figured she could jump right over the water. That wasn't her intention. From beyond the moat of water she intended to speak with the tree.

She took Caspen's hand and they concentrated. *I'm Terra and this is Caspen. I'm not elf but realm walker. I am an abomination, made from a spell that used sacrifice. I am part of the reason for your demise. I'm deeply sorry and want to fix the problem. Please tell me what I need to do.*

For many seconds that felt like minutes the tree did nothing. She considered she should have taken Hank up on his offer. Together, their connection to magic would be stronger. Then a branch shook, and a silver leaf dropped, floating to the water. Small ripples spread across the surface of the moat.

A stream of thought, strong yet weak, passed into her head. *I'm old and your world is dying. You can't fix the wrongs of your ancestors.*

No! That wasn't true. Why did the tree need to sacrifice its life? She could save life and would give her connection to the source willingly. *But I can save you and life.*

Life will begin again. You carry a seed, plant it when the last of my leaves wither.

No! Terra's thoughts paused. How did the tree know she carried a seed? Then again, it didn't really surprise her. The tree was old and the seed a part of it. *I must save those deserving of saving.*

You are noble but others aren't. They seek to destroy. You can't save them. The shadows will grow.

REALM WALKER

The vile one will lead life into destruction and only my death will stop him as he will wither with me.

The tree's words confirmed the Council of Divination, but who was the vile one? There had to be some way to stop him without destroying all life. *If I give myself to the source will that save life and stop the vile one?*

It may, but are you willing to sacrifice all for the lives of those who seek to harm, to end life? The source is growing weak. Your connection to magic is strong, but you must be willing to sacrifice it all in order to save any.

I never asked for what I have. I don't want the connection or to be a godlike being. I desire nothing more than to be a teenager.

The tree chuckled lightly but not in a funny way, more in a 'you don't understand' way. *You will not only give power back to the source and then return as a "normal" teenager. Your life will be gone as your connection to the source is what gives you life. That is the true sacrifice.*

Terra mulled that over in her head. When her mother's soul escaped to Tranquility she felt an energy surge. Distraught at the time, she didn't put it together. The source magic in her didn't return to the source. It went to Terra, yet stayed with her as a soul in the sphere. So if Terra died the magic would return to the source if there was no other realm walker for it to go. She nodded. *Yes, I am willing to give myself, my soul, my life, my heart to the source for the lives of others.*

Then so be it. Silence followed the tree's word stream in Terra's mind as if it disconnected.

Serenity Tree, how do I get to the source?

After a few long seconds the tree responded. *You must solve that on your own, but don't go alone. Take those who are most similar to you. Those you chose, their destinies are intertwined with yours and the warlock. The seven of you must do this alone and be wary of the vile one, for he isn't who you think.*

Knowing she wouldn't get anything more from the tree, who didn't agree with her solution, she disconnected hands with Caspen. The part about the ones she chose, she understood; Alex, Dena, Mario, Warlita and Kenya. She brought them from Lols to serve on the tribunal as diplomats to Lols. The vile one. From the tree's words it was someone she knew. 'He isn't who you think.' The words were present tense.

Caspen's face said so much with his watery eyes and furrowed brows. He didn't agree with her, but understood they had two choices; let life perish or let it thrive. The only solution to save life meant Terra giving her own.

The conversation was gloomy and left Terra with a sense of doom – her doom. She asked Caspen not to mention to the others the part about her dying or the part about the vile one. It wasn't really a sense of duty or making herself a martyr. It was owning up to what she was. The only realm walker in existence. Her kind were sacrificed for much less, yet it was fitting as they were created from the blood and body parts of others. Life from death and death from life.

It was dark by the time she and Caspen returned. Hyacinth had joined Kayln and Hank in the portable. He and Kayln found a spell in one of the scrolls that needed a drop of blood from a pureblood from each realm to perform a spell that would hopefully unblur the words.

Of course, the spell couldn't be performed in Provence since level 3 magic couldn't be used. Once everyone arrived at the portable the plan was to take them to Lols. The only realm a pureblood from each realm could travel, but Terra had a different idea.

17

The blood for the spell had to be given freely, without coercion. Caspen, Kayln, Meesha, and Hyacinth were willing to give. The kink was finding a harvester, troll, and a dragon. Luckily, that wasn't difficult in a land between the realms and they were able to find one of each. It was in a teen's nature to break the rules every so often. The absence of any deceit was needed for the spell to take hold.

That was the second kink. Although Terra found a way around it as they didn't need to discuss the part about the Serenity Tree, only they needed to read the words on the page. Omitting wasn't lying. She'd been practicing that for months with Rosette and her instructors.

Everyone gathered under the tree she made in her private world in the inbetween. The scroll lying on the grass between the group. Hank performed the spell, speaking in warlock, which sounded like gibberish to Terra.

He lifted the dragon's palm over the blurred writing on the scroll and sliced quickly, not deep, but enough to draw blood. The dragon didn't flinch as the blade went across his palm. Hank grabbed the dragon's hand from underneath and rolled his fingers together and squeezed, blood dropped onto the scroll. He did the same with each going clockwise through the realms; Canida, Aradia, Navarin, Verboten, Drakonia, and last, Thraves.

Blood pooled onto the scroll, spreading out in rivulets, like rivers and streams. Last, Hank brought the knife across his palm and squeezed. His blood mingled with that of the others. As it combined, it dissipated and the words beneath cleared.

Terra thanked the purebloods and sent them back. She didn't feel they needed to know the rest. Maybe that was a bit unfair, but that was the way of omitting. She was pleasantly pleased when none of them snarled at her or complained. She also sent her friends back so it wouldn't look like she was singling them out. The plan was to meet in the portable.

From her world in the inbetween she could enter any realm or location. She used this to drop into the portable, unzip the matter surrounding her and walk out.

The scroll lay flat against the table. Her friends seated around the table in their usual spots. Kayln stood as Terra took her place. Her eyes dropped to the large, yellowed with age scroll. "When the moon over Aradia turns silver the seed of the Serenity Tree should be placed in the center of the ascendant where both halves will close over it. The land will swallow the ones who hold the ascendant in their hands." Kayln glanced up. "There's more. To return, the same conditions must apply."

If someone used the ascendant to go to another realm, how would they know from another realm if Aradia's moon was silver? No, there was a way, Terra stopped her thoughts. The moon moved around the realms on a cycle. All they'd need to do was count the days, but that meant they'd be stuck in Marsidia for a month.

She didn't plan on using the ascendant to get to Marsidia. She had the enter stones of Hovrath. Her plan was to use it to get home so they could count how many days had passed since the silver moon and return quicker.

"We only have half the ascendant," Hank announced, his gaze meeting Terra's as if he watched the hamster wheel in her mind spin.

She glanced to her friends who all wore the same expression as Hank. Darn! How had she missed that? Mulling over Kayln's words as she read the script, it was there. The seed goes in the middle of both halves of the ascendant.

Like a gear, Terra's mind clicked into place. Terra knew exactly where to find the other half. She grabbed Hank's hand, feeling hopeful, anxious energy pass from him to her as she portalled them into the storage unit. The light from the portal dissipated quickly, leaving them in the darkness. The room was creepier without any light.

A blue glow illuminated metal objects as a blue light ball moved in front of her. Hank's handiwork. Now they had to find it. There were so many shelves, rows like a grocery store. She took one half and Hank the other.

The blue light Hank created split into two; one followed her as she carefully moved toward the last row, the other followed Hank. The walkways between each row slimmer than a plank. She rounded the edge of the shelf and studied the objects.

The jewelry and metal statues, ancient coins, and the dodecahedrons, an object that looked like an ancient twelve-sided dense metal helmet. That day she hadn't gotten further than the first row. Making sure she hadn't missed it because she wasn't searching for it that day, she scoured each shelf then rounded the corner.

Several rows later, she and Hank landed at the same one in the middle. She took one side and he the other. It had to be there, but she was willing to drop into the professor's office and even home if needed.

"Got it!" Hank announced, a shiny metal object in his hand. Pride and uncertainty muddling his godlike features.

Finally, they had what they needed. Now she needed to gather the five she brought from Lols and find a way to explain to them how they needed to escort her to Marsidia. It was late and tomorrow was a new day.

Clyde slid down Terra's arm as she sat on the edge of her bed. She opened her backpack to take out her elfin history book. Surely it contained information about Serenity Tree. Her hand brushed against a crumpled paper. She hadn't cleaned her bag out in months, not since she unloaded everything into the trunk of the tree.

Pulling it out, it was a sealed envelope, bent and smashed. Curious, she pushed her finger under the sticky part and opened the letter. Inside were two papers. Unfolding them, she studied the top one with an interested eye. They were family trees, dating back to the original seven realm walkers.

Dropping the family tree onto her bed, she ran her fingers along the paper to straighten out the crinkles. Touched with magic, each line grew as she read. Each lineage stopped at one of the twenty-one on the list given to Terra and her friends when they went to Lols to find five tribunal members. Only the eldest born from a realm walker became a realm walker. M'ra's line started with her children as she was an only child. It wasn't a secret she was related to M'ra. Terra just never imagined her giving birth and raising children. Studying the lineage in front of her, she had two children – twins. The oldest, a daughter, followed after her mother as the realm walker but her son eventually left Drakonia for Lols.

M'ra's partner was a fae hybrid, a commoner living in Drakonia. Their son also a fae hybrid. Realm walkers were spelled but carried genes of a hybrid as that's what they were. It made sense that a fae felt out of place in Drakonia. He also wouldn't have fit in Navarin with the snooty fae. At the end of the lineage was Terina.

Terra dropped backwards onto her pillow in a fit of laughter. The door opened and she didn't even notice until Halsey's pitch cut through the airwaves.

"What is wrong with you? Are you drunk on buttons again?"

Halsey's snappy words didn't stop Terra's laughter. She laughed harder as she attempted to rein herself in. "Where's suck-face Bjorn?" she said after several minutes of tempering her fit.

"He's in class." She pushed her closet door open and pulled something out. Terra sat up.

"These ones," Halsey asked, holding up a pair of silver heels, "or these?" She placed the shoes on the floor and picked up a pearly-colored pair.

Both were pure Halsey, and since when did Halsey ask Terra for advice on clothing? A girl who was pleased in sandals or sneakers. Had their relationship developed that much that she trusted Terra's advice? "The pearly ones, but it depends on what you're wearing them with."

"I think so too." Halsey leaned over and laid the shoes on the floor. "Bjorn has something special planned tonight and I want to look perfect."

When *didn't* Halsey think she had to look perfect? Wasn't she always perfect? "I'm taking Clyde for his last stroll of the evening," Terra said, collecting the family trees and making a protective bubble around Clyde as she did when she and Hank trained. No one was kidnapping him ever again.

Realm Walker

Descending the stairs and exiting the school, she thought about the discovery. M'ra was behind it. She'd switched the list the tribunal had with another. That's why the tribunal was confused. It wasn't an act. They were really befuddled. For M'ra it was calculated. No doubt the children and relations of realm walkers, they had some connection beyond others to the realms. Terina knew her father was a warlock, no doubt her mother knew she was a fae-hybrid. How much they understood of their own lineage wasn't clear, but Terina mentioned she moved to Connecticut because of her grandma.

Terra didn't doubt for a second the ripped veil to Navarin in Terina's home was a coincidence, possibly M'ra made the rip herself so her son could travel to and from Navarin, and the land passed from one generation to the next. The enchanted documents found their way into Terra's backpack through Bane. It had his level of secrecy attached.

She sat against a tree and opened the second page. Her forehead wrinkled as her eyes widened. The first lineage was hilarious, but the second was a home run in her gut. The five she'd chosen not on the list were of closer relation to realm walkers than the twenty-one. They were siblings and children of the last realm walkers. Chills coursed her spine like someone dropped ice down her shirt.

Mario was the second son of the Canidan realm walker, Warlita the third daughter of the Verboten realm walker, Kenya the second child an oldest girl of the Navarin realm walker. The chills coursed from her spine to her arms and legs as she read. Alex was the younger brother of the Sier realm walker. He was the one she was most confused about. His predator vision made it possible for him to see even though he was blind. It made sense!

The shock that made every hair on her body stand on end like a cat warding off evil spirits was Dena. She was the younger sister of the Drakonian realm walker – Cyrus' biological father. Dena was Terra's aunt. M'ra told her she sent her to Lols with an elf hybrid couple. That's how she learned to communicate with plants, insects, and animals. Her Drakonian connection, Terra swallowed, is how she understood the basics of the power of suggestion. Her mother wasn't a vampire as that was impossible, they weren't fertile, but was a hybrid from Lols. Terra's body shuddered. She was the first and only daughter of the Thraves and Aradian realm walkers. Together, they covered each realm.

The five were hybrids, deeply connected to the last realm walker. None had trouble visiting other realms. Terra thought it was because they were hybrids like Tania. She went to six realms and Lols. That's why Serenity Tree said she needed to take them. Each had a special connection. Her mind spun like a top on steroids.

Taking deep breaths, she worked to calm the hysteria inside her, when the energy shifted. She paused, instantly going into predator mode. Her senses alert as the energy swung again. With her realm walker vision she watched the matter in her inbetween world slice open. The world she created fluxed and shifted but she couldn't see anyone. The implications stabbing inside her guts. On instinct, she created a portal and vanished in a teal light. Her world light and breezy. She'd never created a moon or stars.

"Who's there?! Show yourself!"

The leaves of the tree blew in the breeze, the golden poppies stood bright and cheery. From a glance, the place didn't appear disturbed. Someone had been there, as impossible as it was. The stones. She hid them in the trunk of the tree.

Curling her finger into her palms in frustration and anxiety, she rushed to the tree. Her mind replaying *still be there…still be there* and stuffed a hand inside, pulling back the matter forming the trunk, her gut clenched. The stones were gone!

"No!" she screamed, turning the breeze into a steady wind that blew her hair over her eyes. "Show yourself!"

In that moment, all her suspicions of the possibility of another realm walker coiled in her mind. Only a realm walker could enter her inbetween world and there was only one possibility of who that realm walker was. Anger brimmed into an inferno as she screamed, a ball of fire flaming from her open mouth, spread through her world.

Realm Walker

18

She writhed in anger as she returned to Provence, tempering the fire inside her. Rebuilding her world helped her gain some perspective and put her mind into solution mode. She paced the perimeter of the campus, Clyde running and bouncing in his protective bubble, her mind a fluster of incoherent thoughts. Her third journey around the campus, the thoughts settled and formed a plan. First, her biological father, Cyrus, was alive. It was the only explanation. There'd been murmurs and suggestions he'd lived through the cleansing and this was her proof.

Only a realm walker could bend matter and energy the way she could. Even a hybrid had limitations. He was clever and hid for decades, but how? And where was he? Now he had the Stones of Hovrath and no doubt would be making the trip, or they were for leverage. If they were for leverage, surely he'd want something in return. *What did he want? Did he have the exit stones?* They vanished after she touched them and before Hank showed up. In order to get them that quick, someone needed the ability to portal or they were hanging out, stalking her.

Bane. *Did he take them?* She was his assignment but had never mentioned anything about them. Would he? She believed he would. Somehow he slipped the envelope of family trees into her bag. He was clever and sly but would he betray it now, after they'd come to some sort of trust? As loyal as he was to M'ra, Terra didn't think so.

Cyrus. It had to be him. Meaning he had passage to Marsidia. Her mind drew a blank. As a realm walker they were an extension of the source. That had more implications than kidnapping the stones, but what did he plan on doing? *Was he willing to sacrifice himself instead of her?*

She didn't think so as he'd stayed hidden all these years, even from her. No, he had something darker planned. She paused for a minute and stamped her feet on the ground. Possibly, he simply didn't want anyone to travel there, which made Terra even more determined.

Clyde stared at her in a frozen stance. Terra tilted her head and studied him. It was unusual for him to be still. "What's up?"

As if waking up from a trance his little eyes shifted to her and he scampered between her feet.

"Pondering the complexities of life is overwhelming," came a male voice from behind her. One she recognized well and didn't expect to see this late at night near the campus.

She swiveled on her heel and faced Gwond. His pouchy belly made him look shorter than he already was. "I'm only pondering the complexities of being *the* only realm walker," she responded. No need to mention how she knew she wasn't the only one.

"That burden is heavy and should be shared."

What did that even mean? Gwond was full of odd sayings that had deep implications. Cyrus snuck into her world. If he was around, hiding and listening, she had words for him. "I wish I had someone to share it with."

He pushed his thick glasses up with his green tail plumage. "Yes, there is strength in numbers. I must be getting home," he excused himself.

She never took for granted his wisdom – *strength in numbers*. Was he implying she needed to rely on others? She did. No, it had a deeper connotation. Shivers ran up her spine as it implied, somehow, that he understood she was planning something. *How?* No, he couldn't know anything. She dismissed the idea.

Too ramped up to sleep, she called everyone together. As her friends arrived, they gathered at the table. She spread out the family trees once everyone arrived, starting with the twenty-one hybrids related to the original seven hybrids. This was how she was going to convince the five to come with her.

Her friends all shared a good laugh when they read the first set of family trees. She'd had the same reaction.

"I have another set to show you but, before I do, I need to explain something." All eyes on her, their giggles sobered as they soaked in her serious tone. "I have to go to Marsidia." None of what she was about to say would surprise Caspen, Kayln, or Hank, but she hadn't told the others what Serenity Tree told her. "The Serenity Tree is dying. In order to save it, I have to give back what I have. My connection to magic."

Kayln pressed a hand to her hip. "You can't give back magic that's created with a blood sacrifice. You'd have to reverse engineer the spell which means more blood."

The bubbly-headed genius. That was the point. Without words, Kayln's face suddenly lost its shine. "Ohhhh!" As she realized Terra was sacrificing herself.

"You can't do that," Hyacinth complained, fighting back tears in her eyes. "The realms need you."

"Life needs me to see that it continues. If I don't do this and Serenity Tree withers completely, shedding its last leaf and bloom, all that we know will be gone. We'll all be gone, and life will start anew."

"What's in that second set?" asked Kinzo cautiously.

Terra continued, "Why we're here." She folded it out and let her friends pile around it. Gasps and ah hahs filled the space. Dena clasped her hand to her mouth and their eyes met. They'd have time for bonding later. "Serenity Tree told me I have to take the five with me. I didn't completely understand then, but I do now. You, like me, are related to cleansed realm walkers. The last realm walkers. I'm all that is left and you are the closest thing to them."

"We don't have to, we're not," Kenya stumbled over her words.

Terra calmed her nervous friends. Not a single one appeared at ease. "No, you aren't realm walkers, but generations of realm walker blood runs through you."

The Ring of Betrayal

The five Lols diplomats she'd chosen and brought to Provence stared at her with unblinking eyes as they considered her words. "The Stones of Hovrath are passage to Marsidia. They've been stolen." She left out the implications that suggested Cyrus, her biological realm walker father, was still alive. They didn't need to know that. "We do have an ascendant which gives us two weeks to plan our trip and we'll be gone for a month..." her words dropped into a void.

She didn't mention any dangers or obstacles they'd face while there. Hank, who sat by her side, had only stories to share as he'd never actually been there. The stories from his ancestors were passed down verbally and all these centuries later were doubtful to be 100% accurate.

Chatter filled the room as the shock wore off. Warlita raised her voice, breaking the tension in the room that was about to snap like a rubber band. "We are Lols diplomats with unique abilities. The job we've been training for is to keep peace between the realms. We have to do this and, if we are successful, then we have earned our place on the tribunal."

She was absolutely correct. The shiver ran up Terra's spine as it had when she ran into Gwond as she paced the school. This is what he meant. They must prove they are worthy of their positions and power.

19

Waiting wasn't a skill Terra held. Two weeks turned into one week. She, Hank, and the five did their best to think of every scenario and practice their magic together. The only positive about waiting was that it gave them the chance to prepare. They'd be stuck there for a month.

A group consisting of a realm walker, a warlock, and five hybrids, they had more than enough abilities between them to face almost any situation that they could think of. She didn't expect the warlocks to be overjoyed they were in Marsidia, yet she thought it prudent they meet with them not sneak through their realm.

The Ring of Betrayal

Using what knowledge he had, Hank explained all the basic types of runes he knew of; invisibility, daylight, darkness, sound, plasma, shields, and silver. The list seemed never ending and on top of all the runes they had endless spells. They practiced counter moves for if they met resistance. It was the most intense practice any of them had experienced since coming to Provence.

The fake sun lowered in the Provence sky as they returned and gathered in the portable. Hank drew a map of Marsidia using a spell. Lines moved across the parchment, displaying tree-covered highlands and waterfalls dropping into a series of rivers that crossed the valley. Names of towns and places scrolled across the tops of what appeared to be homes and farms. The valley was large and in the center was the source. It was shown as a great ball with vertical and horizontal lines around it displaying its brightness. It reminded Terra of a sun on the ground or the blob on the dungeon wall in Navarin.

The realm seemed smaller than the others. It puzzled her why she couldn't see Marsidia if it existed. Was it part of the realm walker design? Would Merla have known of Marsidia? She revamped the warlock spell to create the curtains, veils, Provence, and realm walkers. It seemed she may have had knowledge of Marsidia, even if limited.

Realm Walker

Thoughts of Merla turned her mind to Kayln who knew spells. She was a top-level spell caster who could speak and read old fae fluently. The top of her class. According to Kayln, spells could be reversed. Is that why she needed the grimoire? Did she need to take it with her?

She and Hank were the last in the portable to leave. She pushed her chair out to stand. He grabbed her hand. "I know we have a job to do together as a team but I have…" He paused, his beautiful dark eyes searching hers. "As a warlock I have questions that need answers."

Of course he did and he should get those answers. She was curious herself. "Knowledge you can bring back to the Lols warlocks?"

He nodded then brought her hand up, cupping both of his around it. "Not only that and maybe not that. I need to know why warlocks were locked out of their lands. Was it the fae? Everything we've learned leans towards the warlocks in Marsidia locking the other warlocks out. The grimoire… I don't think its fae, or at least not wholly fae, but warlock too."

Terra rested her chin against his cupped hands. More than probably anyone alive, she understood. She was unique in what she was and, piece by piece, learned more and more what it was to be a realm walker and the depth of the intense command of magic she had. Now there was another and she needed to find him, not because he was her biological father, but because he held the answers to questions she wanted to understand. Hearing about the cleansing always made her skin crawl and her heart crack, but she never heard his reason or his part in the injustice that wiped out realm walkers. Was he as M'ra described: a victim? Or was he the perpetrator? There were always two sides and rarely was anything clear cut.

She wanted to believe Cyrus was a victim, but then why did he steal the Stones of Hovrath? These were answers she needed before giving herself to the source, not that they would change anything. How had she been upset at Hank for not completely trusting her? He was questioning everything he'd learned growing up. No longer following blindly. Same as Terra. She pretended to be an elf, went to Lols to bring back five diplomats from their list but ended up choosing her own five. A list of descendants of the original realm walkers or their siblings. Merla's spell said no harm could come to realm walkers, but it didn't specify their families couldn't be banished. Was that how they went to Lols? Or did they go willingly, unable to fit in with a body of purebloods? The five she brought back were descendants of those banished after the cleansing because of their blood relationship to the realm walkers.

Terra figured that was a blessing in disguise. Losing someone was painful. Losing someone because they were murdered out of fear was wrong. They'd have daily reminders of what the realms did and that hate would build into revenge. Their families still in Lols, were they surprised their children vanished or had they expected one day it would happen?

Hank kissed her fingertips, drawing her away from her thoughts. A hormone-induced wave traveled through her hand and rested in her heart. In that weak moment, she pressed her lips to his. The explosion of fireworks inside her went off like a finale on New Year's Eve. Through the fireworks, a silhouette appeared: tall, slender. She couldn't tell if the person was wearing a hood or had long hair. As their lips parted, the vision dissolved. Not willing to let go yet, she put her hand around his neck and pulled him closer, pressing her lips against his.

Was the vision real time or past tense? She hadn't felt the pull of the veils and the beat always inside her remained steady. It had given her hope they wouldn't be too late. In truth, she had no connection to Marsidia.

The silhouette reappeared and a blinding light passed over her closed eyes, bursting inside her head, thrusting her and Hank apart. They dropped into their seats from the air. The kiss levitating them. A sharp pain thrust upward from her tailbone as she hit the wooden seat.

What had she seen? Was the silhouette the vile one or was it one of the shadows from the Council of Divination? "Did you see that?"

Hank rubbed his tail bone. "It hurt coming down."

She shook her head and jumped to her feet. "No, the light. It forced us apart."

He lowered his brows. "What light?"

"We have to go." She couldn't explain, but her thoughts streamed to Serenity Tree. It was as if the tree was in distress. She picked up Clyde, who climbed to her shoulder, and cut the fabric of Provence open. Glancing to her side she asked Hank, "Are you coming?"

They stepped out of the swirling teal matter, feet from the watery moat around the tree. Solaflies hovered on the edge of the moat, their light shining on the surface of the water. The tree's branches hung low as if it was hard work to hold them up. Its trunk looked shrunken since her visit only a week ago.

Terra jumped over the moat, landing beside the shrunken trunk of the majestic tree. She wrapped her arms in a hug around it. *How can I help you? Please tell me.*

REALM WALKER

It is too late, the tree said in a tired, weary voice, as if it was difficult to talk.

No! It's never too late. Is it the vile one or the shadows? Is that what I saw? How do I get to Marsidia? Is there another way besides the ascendant and the stones?

The tree rested a branch on her empty shoulder and Clyde climbed onto it. *So many questions. The ascendant will not take you to Marsidia.* Terra's hopes instantly plummeted to the ground and shattered, barely hearing the tree's next words. *You are a realm walker there is nothing to keep you out of any realm.*

Terra's brain did a double take, repeating the tree's words. *But I don't see it or feel it. How do I find it?*

Yes, you do. That's why you are here. Look down and let go. Marsidia you will find.

Terra dropped her hands from the tree and glanced down at a reflection of herself in the mirrored surface of the water, pondering the tree's words. She leaned further over, her reflection vanishing, the water appearing dark and endless. *Through the water?*

The tree didn't respond in words. Lowering its branch over her back, a single leaf dropped, descending to the moat where it gently rested upon the water.

20

The urgency of the dire situation forced Terra to collect the five and take them to Aradia. There would be no goodbyes or Hyacinth hugs before taking the journey. However, she had taken Kayln's unsolicited and accidental advice and stuffed the grimoire in her backpack, along with the ascendant and her mother's tiara. Maybe it wouldn't get them to Marsidia but could help them travel the realm.

It was about as perfect a spring day as she'd ever seen. The sun was bright, wispy clouds spread high in the sky, and a slight breeze swept over them. Color sprung from every plant. It was difficult for Terra to imagine a world where all the beauty was destroyed and left as wastelands.

Dena's round face was absent a smile and etched in worry. Normally, she was a bubbly person but had been on edge since learning *who* she was. They had discussions about Cyrus, but Terra didn't have much to offer and hadn't mentioned she thought he was alive. With Dena's apprehensions she didn't want to add to the list.

Dena pushed the sleeves of the thin, baby blue sweater she was wearing over her elbows. A girl who wore skirts every day, she was more practically dressed for the excursion in a white and blue polka-dot skort.

Warlita stared down at the water's surface. Bangles pressing against each other with a jingle as she brushed a few strands of bright red hair behind her ear. As requested, she'd also worn more practical clothing with jeans and a light jacket, although Terra would have ditched her shoes - a pair of cheetah print boots. They were Warlita. "We're jumping into that?" she asked with a sneer.

Yes. It was simple and she felt no more need to explain. They'd been on this journey with her since she brought them to Provence.

"The Serenity Tree is wise. You must trust her," Caspen responded, relieving Terra of the burden of once again explaining Marsidia was below the tree. On a level she didn't understand, it didn't surprise her. She understood the stones created a path of nourishment for the tree after the veils were formed and sealed. Strife killed the tree and all that added up to Marsidia, the realm below the tree, below the realms.

Caspen had the difficult job of breaking the news to the others that they were gone. The mission had to be expedited on account of the tree's frailty. Sure, Hyacinth would be upset, Meesha would understand, Kinzo and Nalysse who knew, and Kayln pouty. It also saved Terra from having to part ways knowing she wouldn't make it back, yet something nibbled at Terra's brain and her heartfelt farewell wasn't forever with her friends. Somehow, someway, she'd see them again, but with Rosette it was different. Probably the questioning adult eye that didn't always trust Terra, knowing she often had her own motives and agenda. It also would have looked weird her saying goodbye to Rosette without any explanation.

Terra's mind returning to the present, she wasn't sure exactly how the water led to Marsidia. For all she knew, Marsidia was upside down or a completely different dimension, or maybe she'd drop from a cloud in the sky.

Kenya clucked her tongue and moved closer to her best friend Warlita, eyes focused on the still water. Dressed in her usual black, pants instead of a skirt and fishnets or purposely ripped tights. Her dark curls pulled back in a ponytail. "Who goes first?"

"You will all follow me and Hank will go last." Terra would have been happy to give Hank the opportunity to go first but she felt it was her duty as the realm walker. Sure, Hank had the rune and the others were children of realm walkers, but could they go on their own? Did she open some type of portal or passage by going first?

Warlita's head still hung over the glassy surface of the water. Kenya pushed against her back and Warlita wobbled then clutched Kenya's arm, who was laughing so hard she stumbled backward.

"This isn't a game," Dena chided. "Stop goofing off before someone falls in."

Terra held in a laugh as it was funny to watch Kenya and Warlita bobble on the edge. Dena was uptight.

Mario's hair had grown and fell midway down his back in a mixture of waves and curls. He always dressed practical in jeans and T-shirts. "I made a choice to leave my family and my home to be a diplomat. If that means I have to travel to this unknown realm to fulfill my duty than that's what I will do." His words made Terra's heart burst. She wasn't alone, never had been. They were like her, commoners whose job was to keep peaceful relations between the realms, including Marsidia.

Alex stayed quiet. His short, golden hair trimmed neatly above his ears, cargo shorts and a polo shirt on. He'd dressed like Alex but did switch out his sliders or crocs for laced sneakers.

Terra moved to the edge of the water, Clyde scampering beside her. She glanced down at him, not sure what to expect once she went below the surface. "You ready?" she asked, not expecting Clyde to react the way he did as he jumped into the water.

His little head disappearing below the surface, her heart did a double beat in anxiety than quelled as she plunged in after him. The water was tepid against her skin as she dropped into it. Roots swam out of the way giving her a straight shot down.

Her eyes found Clyde a few feet away, swimming downward as if he knew where he was going. The deeper she went the darker it got and his form was more difficult to see until she couldn't. Reminding herself the tree was wise, she pushed the panic she felt creeping in her gut away. She could easily create an air bubble as she did in Navarin when they followed the disturbance to the bottom of the ocean floor, but she was a decent swimmer and so was Clyde.

The world turned and she became disoriented until light shone through the water. Swimming towards it, she drew her head above its surface, glancing around for Clyde like an anxious mother. The tide pushed her body as she treaded water. It flowed from high and vanished into the trees.

Colors spread across the sky in waves, just as Hank described: pink, purple, and blue, edged in a silver glow. No, not as he described but more breathtaking than he described.

Fog rose through the trees surrounding the river and her but they stopped before reaching the high canopy of leaves. Not all realms had green leaves on trees, Marsidia did but unlike in any other realm they glowed. There was no sun. The only light was from the waves of color making up the sky and the trees. The air smelled of scents unfamiliar to her. The closest thing she could think of was honeysuckle, yet not as sweet.

A wet Clyde swam towards her and climbed onto her head then chittered at her as if trying to get her attention. "What?"

His tail swung over her eyes like wet windshield wipers. She pushed it away and turned her head. The river ended only a few feet from her position. *Shit!*

She formed a bubble around her and Clyde as they dropped over the edge, falling many feet. Her stomach caught and stayed several feet in the air, finally catching up to her as the protective bubble reached the ground.

It hit the rocks below with a gentle bounce. Clyde was climbing down from her head and onto her shoulder when screaming caught her attention. She glanced upward, seeing only rushing water pouring over the fall.

She'd been so taken with Marsidia's beauty she'd forgotten they weren't alone. Pushing the protective energy bubble upward, it caught Kenya as she dropped over the edge. "I got you!" Terra screamed, hoping Kenya heard her over the rush of the water.

Kenya met her gaze as the energy lowered her slowly next to Terra. "What about them?" She pointed upward.

Terra extended the bubble outward, catching them all as they scrambled to swim against the current. "Go with it!" she yelled.

One by one, they dropped over the edge. Her bubble molded around them, landing each safely like someone jumping onto a huge inflatable trampoline.

She solidified the energy like a bridge and they walked over the stream. They'd dropped from the tallest waterfall but there were several more every several yards or so. From where she stood she couldn't see how far down the falls went until the river leveled out, which meant they were high in the mountains.

Realm Walker

Marsidia wasn't a cold place. Even in the highlands the air didn't feel cold against her wet skin and soggy clothing.

"It really exists…" Dena said as she stepped onto the shore, her head tilted upward as if exploring the tops of the trees or the colorful sky. Her voice no longer filled with trepidation but wonder.

Warlita handed Terra a bracelet. "I planned on giving these to everyone before we made the plunge, but you jumped in," she said in a scolding tone. Terra took the bracelet. "They are like a magic GPS and will help us find each other if someone should get lost or we get separated."

"Thank you." Terra slipped the bracelet onto her wrist. It was a simple, bronze-colored metal. She noted everyone else already had one on.

"Where now?" Mario asked, wringing out his long, dark, wet locks.

Hank already had the map pulled out and laid on the ground. Each had a backpack filled with tricks of their trade and food. Terra brought extra, as she had to feed Clyde who was running in circles and rolling all over the glowing grass.

The glowing grass crunched as the group joined Hank and they half-glanced at the map as they couldn't stop studying the amazing world around them. "I think we are here at Tripper Falls and if we go," he drew a line with his finger to show direction, "to the east we'll end up here at Vonester Run."

"That's where we'll find warlocks?" Dena asked with hesitation.

He glanced up from the map. "We should. It's a town."

It felt like a good time for Terra to inform the group of what she'd kept from them, or at least a better time than after meeting the warlocks who might not be friendly towards them. She addressed the group and watched their expressions twist with a variety of emotions. "Before we set out, I need to warn all of you I think I know who stole the Stones of Hovrath and I don't know if he's a friendly or an enemy. It might not be him. It could be the vile one or the shadows from the Council of Divination, but I don't think they could have gone into my secret world."

Kenya jutted out her hip and rested a hand against it. "Spit it out."

Terra glanced to Dena who swallowed hard, knowing the direction Terra was headed. The realm walker brother she never met. Shifting her gaze to Kenya who was impatient, she explained, "Cyrus, my biological father. He's the only person who could have possibly snuck into my secret world since he's a realm walker and all…" Her words dropped off.

"There's another one of you?" Kenya snorted.

"Yeah, but I've never met him. In fact, I thought he was dead." Terra pushed her foot over the rocks. "His soul was never harvested according to the harvesters and M'ra, the former Drakonian Minister, believed he was alive." She stopped there, the pain of losing M'ra still burned and she didn't feel like going down the rabbit hole of the past few months of her life.

Dena asked, "Why would he do that?" in a tone that suggested she'd heard the pain and hesitation in Terra's voice and shared it. It was hard to hide things from someone who had the ability to use words and the power of suggestion as well as a biological connection.

"I don't know. I thought maybe he didn't want anyone else here in Marsidia, but I had a vision the other day. A silhouette of someone here in Marsidia. It was dark and they didn't look familiar, then something bright burst and blew them backwards."

Hank stopped rolling the map and turned to Terra with a knowing glance. When they'd kissed she'd seen the vision but hadn't elaborated. The expression on his face showed he wished she had.

Kenya rolled her eyes. "And you waited until now to tell us this?!"

Sure, Terra would be upset too and probably react about the same way.

Sliding the backpack over his shoulder, Hank said, "I didn't know either. It doesn't matter so long as we are careful. I don't think it will take us more than a couple hours to reach Vonester Run by foot."

"Why don't we use magic? It's everywhere and thick," Alex suggested.

Terra and Hank's gazes met and silently said words they'd previously spoken. Terra let Hank handle that one, having given the group enough bad news. "We aren't in Provence or any of the known realms. No one has been in or out of Marsidia in millennia. If we use magic, it might alert the warlocks and be seen as a threat."

Realm Walker

21

The group of seven strolled single file through the forest. The glow from the tree leaves lit the way, but there was no path or trail. The fog grew denser the further in they went until their vision was limited. Terra's mind swirled with thoughts as she attempted to make out where everyone was through the thick fog.

Clyde chose to walk instead of ride on Terra's shoulder. She'd brought his harness to keep him close in this strange land. Through the fog, he was difficult to see, but she could make out his form and little ears. He'd run ahead then pause, turn his head to the left, then run again. His brown-tipped ears twitched every so often and he'd make quiet noises as he checked out this new realm.

The Ring of Betrayal

Before setting out on their journey across the highlands, Terra used her realm walker vision to *see* Marsidia. The highlands surrounded the valley in a circle and, judging by the lines over the edges of the land, it was shaped like a sphere that didn't extend further beyond the highest peaks of the mountain.

The village they were marching toward wasn't far. At some point, they'd have to cross a stream, and once over the stream they were in Vonester's Run. From what she could make out, it wasn't much but a few square structures that reminded her of a medieval village with a pub, a few houses, horses, and farmland. Only there wasn't much land to farm. The area around the stream was solid and rocky and the town appeared as if they'd chopped down the trees, and cleared a small area and left the rest. Each structure had maybe enough land for a personal garden.

She searched for the source, but found nothing that stood out. The air was thick with magic, like Alex said, and it made things fuzzier and harder to see, making no sense to Terra who thought being closer to the source would make it easier. Across the valley that was completely covered in a blanket of fog, was a strange patch of violet light. At first, she thought it was the source, only the source was supposed to be in the valley not the mountains.

Realm Walker

Dena joined Terra. "I can barely tell where we are. Maybe we should stop until the fog clears."

She had a point. They'd been traveling for a couple hours and didn't appear any closer to Vonester's Run than when they began. Using her realm walker vision, she found the village. It was the only village remotely close, which is how she figured out it was the right one. Any others she'd spotted weren't close, nor were they easy to see.

Terra stopped. Dena kept walking until she realized Terra wasn't moving anymore. "Terra." Her voice almost a panic.

When Terra responded, Dena walked towards her until she could see her again. "What do you see?"

She wasn't sure what she saw or how to explain it or whether it was the magic messing with her. Biting at the inside of her mouth she released then yelled to the group. "Stop walking and gather around me."

The footsteps and crunching leaves were easier to hear than to see their forms moving towards her. Hank finding his way to her side, she grimaced before telling them the bad news, hoping they didn't see her disappointment. "The magic in the air distorts things, but I'm sure we haven't gotten any closer to the village."

Kenya clucked her tongue and snapped, "What?! We've been walking for hours and haven't gone anywhere? How is that possible?"

Warlita mumbled her woes, seconding anything Kenya said. They were best friends in Lols, roommates at Provence Academy, and Warlita followed anything Kenya did, usually. Terra was sure they even shared clothes on occasion. Kenya was a couple inches shorter than Warlita and had a bit thicker build but otherwise they were close in size.

Soon grumbles erupted, aimed at Hank who only knew stories passed down through the generations. Like the rest of them, this was his first time in Marsidia, the home warlocks had been trying to get back to. He'd been close-lipped about it and Terra couldn't tell if he was excited or worried. She figured he'd come around when he was ready.

"There are no stories about travel here being different than any other realm. I suppose it could be, but I don't understand how we've been walking and haven't gotten any further." Hank's voice was soft but edged in confusion. He had no answers.

"We're surrounded by thick magic. It could be playing tricks on us," Mario inserted, glancing toward Terra.

Through the blanket of suspended water, she barely made out that he turned his head.

"Or travel could be different," Alex's voice cut through the group and some of the fog cleared. "The fog could be a hint."

A shelf of fog collided with Terra and she fell backwards onto it. Expecting to fall, she landed on a pillowy shelf of fog next to Alex, her feet dangling over the edge. She gently tugged at the leash of the harness and caught Clyde as he jumped onto the fog shelf. Her fingers went through the fog but it held her butt in place. Smoothing the droplets of water, she poked little holes in the fog. It quickly moved and filled them in.

"How did you do that?" Dena asked, standing in front of Alex and Terra.

"Easy, think it."

Hank leaned back on the fog shelf Terra sat on with Alex and it caught him. Slowly the fog cleared and bunched into shelves for everyone to ride on.

Hank chuckled lightly. "Vonester was a recluse with a rune that controlled water. He also controlled electricity and made storms without rain but with droplets of water that hung in the air. A small group came with him and that's how Vonester's Run came to be."

Bangles clanged together as Warlita raised her arm. "Why didn't you tell us that earlier?" she griped as she pushed a chunk of red hair wet from the fog behind her ear.

"Would it have made a difference?" Hank snapped in return.

"Arguing won't solve anything. How do we steer the clouds?" Dena asked.

Terra knew the answer, but Alex beat her to it. "We think it."

Alex was turning out to be the most help so far. He saw things the others didn't, like Terra, only different.

The clouds didn't appear to move, yet within a minute they carried them over the stream and they were staring at the clearing and few structures that made up the whole of Vonester's Run. The creek was smaller even than Terra thought, as a thin trickle of water ran downhill towards a fall and dropped over the edge. The rocks surrounding the stream and in the stream were black with shiny crystals. Each crystal worn smooth by erosion. They twinkled as the fog rolled over them and became thick, hanging fog as each jumped off their fog shelf.

An eerie feeling crept over Terra as they weren't greeted. The village was silent and empty. A total of eight buildings made up the village. Each square, none standing out over another, and made from logs and thatched roofs. Changing her opinion, the place reminded her less of a medieval village and more like a pioneer settlement in North America.

They split up. Mario, Alex, and Dena taking three houses, Warlita and Kenya taking two, and Hank and Terra taking two more.

They would meet up at the eighth. Hank pushed the door open as it wasn't even locked, nor did it have a lock. Inside, the little structure was more than she guessed and far more modern than it appeared from the outside.

They entered a large room with a fluffy couch that looked perfect for jumping on. There was a bedroom on either side, and a kitchen in the back. The place didn't look big enough for all the room inside – magic. The table in the kitchen had five chairs and five plates with settings of silverware and glasses. A covered basket lay on the middle of the table. Cautiously, Terra lifted the cover on the basket, revealing biscuits. A pot sat on a stove, only it wasn't like any stove she'd ever seen. It had burners but no knobs or buttons to push and below it was an oven door with a window and no handle.

She cocked her head as she studied the odd appliance and waved her hand in of front it, tapped on it, blew on it, snapped her fingers and nothing happened. '*Think it.*' Alex's words came to her mind. *Warm up the stew,* she thought, projecting it towards the oven. The burner beneath it didn't light up, but when she pressed her hand against the pot it was warm. *Stop warming the stew,* she thought, then took a couple steps backwards and turned around curling her fingers over the top of a chair.

The Ring of Betrayal

Magic. Everything here worked with magic. The glasses on the table were mostly full and there wasn't a coating of thick dust. She pulled out the chair and thought with her elbows on the table and hands pressed against her cheeks. Why was the table set and food prepared on the stove, yet no one was around? Who would leave a meal and why? She was perplexed.

Hank interrupted her thoughts as he came into the kitchen with its modern style and enchanted appliances and pulled out a chair across from her.

He had no words. By the look on his face, he was flustered. His eyebrows were flat and full lips tight.

"Someone was here. Not long ago. The food is cold. Why would someone leave it?"

He shrugged. "All my life I've heard about Marsidia and it's exactly like the stories passed down, but something feels wrong. It could be that I'm doing this without other warlocks, or that the stones were stolen and someone else who doesn't belong is here with us…" His words trailed off.

Someone here that didn't belong. Exactly. The magic was heavy and, as newbies to the realm, they had no idea yet how to command it. It was more likely to her that the warlocks left in a hurry and were watching them from afar. In the back of her mind were thoughts of Cyrus, but she still couldn't think of any reason for him to be in Marsidia. Only when her brain solved that puzzle would it make sense. "The warlocks built this place up in your mind and now you're here and it's empty. I think we should mount our clouds and travel further in."

His eyes glanced away from her and towards the great room in the middle. "No one has entered or left Marsidia in thousands of years. I guess they could be taking precautions."

Her logical side figured they were safe, but the vision she saw during their kiss was still front and center in her mind. She couldn't shake it. Who did she see? *The vile one?* Who even was the vile one? The shadows? She stood and pushed in her chair. "Let's look at the other house."

The next house was pretty much the same – empty, with signs that someone had been there sometime recently. Her mind returned to the travel thing. They'd walked and walked with no progress, but the fog shelves didn't seem to move and they were in Vonester's Run. So far, she hadn't used any magic except the protective bubble that saved everyone from the fall. The energy and magic buzzed in the air around her as if she could make it do anything. Hank warned her not to and she'd respected his wishes…so far.

The Ring of Betrayal

Hank and Alex went into the last house as the rest chilled outside and shared food they'd stuffed into their bags. Terra handed out beef jerky, one of her favorite protein staples, and others handed out dried fruit and drinks. She poured a small bowl of food for Clyde and water.

From her spot, she could see the stream and the crystal rocks, reminding her of the crystals and metals in the caves of Sier. The waves of color in the sky reminded her of the colorful ribbons of Verboten, the glowing plants like Aradia and its sarcanthum flowers and solaflies. The magic in the air was like the fairy dust circulating against the golden skies of Navarin. It was as if each realm was made from a slice of Marsidia's magic.

The eighth house held no surprises. Hank sat on the edge of a bench and took a strip of jerky from Terra as she spun around on her butt and faced him, sitting cross-legged on the sandy dirt in front of him. His hands clasped together as he leaned his elbows against his thighs. She wrapped her hands around his and pressed her head against his knee.

There was nothing she could say to make this better for him, but her heart ached. This was his life's dream. All the questions he had might not get answered if they didn't find any warlocks to answer them.

REALM WALKER

They took a vote and decided it wasn't practical or safe to stay in Vonester's Run. They knew nothing of the wildlife, having yet to see any, and less of the warlocks. Normally she could find life forms, but the thick magic interfered with her command of magic.

The thick fog condensed into shelves and they sat, Hank studying his map, turning it in various directions.

Mario pointed. "Through the trees." He commanded his fog shelf forward. Warlita and Kenya met each others' gaze, shrugged, and followed him. Terra didn't see anything but trees ahead, but she trusted his acute predator senses and commanded her cloud to follow Mario.

Hank folded the map and followed behind the group. Glancing over her shoulder, Terra couldn't help feeling horrible for Hank, his face distraught and his shoulders drooping.

He was tall, thin, yet muscular. A majestic specimen of a male. His head lowered, he wasn't himself. Disappointment was written all over him as if someone had used a permanent marker.

By the time Terra turned around, they were at their destination. Mario was off his shelf, sniffing the air. In front of them was an entrance to a cave. The circular opening through the jagged stones was dark like the rocks by the river and tiny embedded crystals shimmered.

"We should stay here and rest," Mario said, stuffing his hands into his pockets.

The fog lingered outside the cave as they entered. Without using magic, Terra pulled the cell phone out of her pocket and turned on the flashlight. The walls were smooth, with rough crystals jutting from the rock. Larger crystals than the ones outside or by the stream. She pressed her hand to one. Vibrations ran through her in waves that spread out as they neared her feet and absorbed into the ground. She pulled her finger away.

Clyde curled up next to her as she pressed her back against the wall and closed her eyes. It hadn't seemed like any time had passed when her eyes popped open. They quickly found Mario, Warlita, and Kenya asleep across from her. The space wasn't large, and their feet nearly touched hers. Hank was beside her, his head tilted in an awkward position that looked uncomfortable. Outside were voices. It was the voices that woke her.

The only person missing was Alex. Rising without disturbing Hank, she carefully stepped over everyone's legs making her way to the entrance of the cave, Clyde joining her as she stared into the heavy fog.

Squinting her eyes, she made out two fuzzy forms; the familiar, tall, thin, form of

Alex, the other larger, broader shoulders, with a cloak hanging over him. The length of it ran to his feet where he wore blue tennis shoes.

She held in a chuckle. The cloak looked like something from another time, but the blue shoes were modern. They didn't go together, which is why his attire caught her attention.

"Terra. You should join us," Alex said, without even turning his head, but why would he? He was blind and the disability, as well as his connection to Sier, gave him other abilities. She ducked to avoid the jagged rocks and stepped out of the cave.

The suspended water droplets spread out and swirled around them, encapsulating the three. The hood of the man's cloak hung over his head and all she could see of his face was the tip of his nose and mouth.

"I'm Sulien, the last of the warlocks."

22

lex stood tall and straight, facing the warlock. "I was explaining how we got here without the stones."

Sulien faced Terra, but she was unable to see more of his face as it was shadowed by the cloak. Slices of recognition teased her mind. "I've been told since the day I was born the warlocks would return. I've expected it all my life. But you aren't warlocks?"

Terra introduced herself before responding to his question. "No, but we bring one with us who has heard stories of Marsidia."

Sulien explained how, over time, the warlocks died as insanity took over. Before the realm was closed they came and went, but once the realm was closed having no way out and being this close to the source they slowly went mad, unable to tell reality from fiction and unable to make anything happen. *The magic is thicker as one gets closer to the source. Like radiation*, Terra thought.

His explanation made sense yet, if that was true, why wasn't he mad like the others? Why was there relatively fresh food and seating for five at the house? She thought to question it then decided to keep her mouth shut. Maybe he was mad and only seemed sane. She did ask about the houses, since it seemed they hadn't been unoccupied for long. He blamed the magic, explaining how it does strange things on its own.

It wasn't long before the rest woke up and joined them outside the cave, the fog moving and swirling around them. Was Sulien commanding the fog or was it doing it on its own?

Hank watched him with a cautious eye and Terra could see the wheels in his mind spinning with every question he had to ask, yet he kept tight-lipped.

It was Sulien who said, answering one of the questions on Terra's mind, "I have never left this realm. I was the only warlock born after the realms were sealed, which may be the reason I didn't go insane as the others did." His face sullen, he continued, "I am happy to have the company, but I must warn you, you mustn't stay long, as the magic may drive you to madness."

They didn't plan on staying long, only long enough for Terra to save the tree and life. The group fell silent and all eyes fell on Terra, except Hank's, who didn't take his eyes off the warlock. He studied him like a detective examining a crime scene. Hank's tone smooth as melted butter: "We came through the roots of the Serenity Tree. It's dying and without it all life will perish. Its roots are somehow blocked and connected to the source. We need to find the source and save the tree. Once we do that we will return home."

Sulien's head turned to Hank. Other than his lack of a smile, Terra couldn't see his facial expression. "Warlocks are guardians of the source. I alone protect it. Although it needs little protecting, as the closer one gets to it the more dangerous it is. It is impossible to get close unless it wants you there. If your plan is to save this tree you must ask the source for permission and it must be granted."

"Then that's what we'll do," Terra stated, not mentioning that she was an extension of the source. Dying was always on the table and it wasn't appealing. She wasn't the type to be a martyr, but hadn't seen any other option. Her mother had given her life so Terra could live. It was time for Terra to repay. A life for a life. His words gave her some hope that maybe the source would allow her to live.

"It's a long journey to the source and not an easy one. Marsidia is filled with pitfalls. You must eat first," Sulien said, picking a handful of leaves from the tree to his side. He folded his hands around the leaves and dropped them. As they fell, each leaf turned into food on a plate. The plates halted in front of them, each holding a different food. In front of Terra was an English muffin with an egg in the middle and melted cheese falling over the sides. "You must use something to turn it into something else. The magic knows what it is you want," he explained as the group eyed their plates skeptically.

Warlita picked up the slice of pizza on her plate and stared at it for a minute before folding it and taking a bite. "This is delicious!" she announced, after swallowing her bite and stuffing the slice back into her mouth for a second.

Terra had never thought of using magic to create food. It gave her a new perspective on her abilities. If she was an extension of the source she could literally mold anything she wanted out of existing matter. New clothes, shoes, anything her mind thought of. She had stopped with the creation of her private world, but why when she could do so much more? Molding the magic in front of her she made a glass and filled it with sweet, pulpless OJ.

Hank elbowed her side gently as a reminder to not use magic, but now that they found a warlock why not use it? She shot him a quick *why not* glance, hoping Sulien wouldn't catch it.

Kenya smiled and chanted something under her breath. The enchanted air in front of her swirled and a bubbling soda appeared. "That is so cool!" she said, holding the glass and studying the effervescent liquid.

It wasn't long before they were all playing with magic in their own way, except Hank, who was far more cautious.

Sulien eyed them curiously as he explained the path to the source and the dangers. "We will only be able to ride the fog to the fog line that hangs over the valley, after that we will have to walk and ride the falls as I don't have a fog rune." He paused. "Both of those can be dangerous. Not much wildlife lives above the fog, but below the fog are water serpents, manticores, Pegasus, and griffons and all of them will fight to keep anyone from reaching the source, even warlocks."

"Why isn't there wildlife above the fog?" Mario asked.

Kenya guffawed before Sulien could respond. "Manticores and griffons. You expect us to believe that?"

Sulien ignored her, answering Mario's question. "They don't like the wet air," Sulien stated as he formed the fog into a seat and sat. "Come," he commanded, and the fog moved into seats for everyone. Kenya rolled her eyes and let out an audible sigh as she sat back onto the fog seat.

They used the fog to get to Vonester's Run, they used it to leave the cave. Within moments, they were on the mountain where the fog met the blanket that hung over the valley, making it impossible to see below.

Terra had created a safe bubble and was sure she could do it again to get to the valley, but didn't want to further upset Hank who remained wary and silent. His lack of words and expression gave her the impression he was concerned.

The fog shelves dissipated around them and joined and clung to the blanket over the valley. "We have to walk through the shelf. Once on the other side of it you will be able to see the valley, but must watch for the Pegasus. They are beautiful but vicious. Their wings have a span of several meters and they are powerful and will use the downdrafts created by them to knock you off balance and keep you unsteady. It can be nearly impossible to keep your footing. If we are quiet we may be able to slip by them," Sulien warned, a lavender lightning cord extending from his palms.

Dena stepped back. "What are you doing with that?"

"You have a warlock among you. The first rune we all receive is plasma. If he will combine his powers with mine the plasma will bind us together so no one plummets to their death," his words firm.

Hank nodded, extending a plasma cord.

"Seriously?" Kenya stepped next to Dena, arms folded over her chest. "How do we know you aren't going to use it to throw us to the valley or feed us to the manticores?"

Sulien squared his shoulders. "You complain and don't believe? Move through the fog line and see with your eyes," he said, taking two fingers and pointing them towards her face.

Warlita surprised Terra as she stepped away from Kenya who was being a royal pain and planted her feet firmly into the ground. It was like her to be stubborn and question things, but not to be overly defiant when it came to something new. She had an adventurous spirit. The only reason Terra could think is that she was scared and definitely not the type who would show fear as she'd be afraid of showing weakness.

"You are in Marsidia, my home, and you question me? Did I invite you? Have I been helping you? I could have easily left all of you in the cave or wandering the mountain for days, never finding your way through the fog."

Kenya rolled her eyes as Sulien's words sank into her hardheaded brain. She sighed, then snapped with a word of warning, "Fine, but don't try anything. I have magic too."

Sulien chuckled as he wrapped a plasma cord around her. "You don't understand Marsidia." His words harsh, giving Terra chills.

Were they doing the right thing? Should they be trusting the warlock? Hank clearly didn't. It wasn't wise to show a blatant mistrust of him as he was right: they didn't understand Marsidia. Terra, though, considered herself a secret weapon. She could easily mold anything into anything she needed or wanted, including a bubble that would safely envelop or catch them like she had when they fell into the river.

Everyone bound together by plasma, Sulien wound it around a tall tree with fire engine red leaves, its trunk several feet thick. He lowered himself, his bottom half disappearing through the blanket of fog, his hands clutching the rocks. "You must follow my path in a single file line and don't speak."

Terra followed behind him as she thought if anything went awry it would be best for the group as she'd be able to mold the magic into anything she wanted. Her feet found the rocks below as she clutched the one jutting out of the mountain, barely able to see the top of Sulien's cloak. She was glad the fog was so thick that she couldn't see how far the valley below was.

Warlita followed behind her, noted by her animal print boots. Clutching the rocks tight, it was slow going as her feet searched for the next set of rocks to stand on. It seemed silly, in a land of magic, that they were climbing down rocks instead of using the magic. Were there no caves that took them into the valley or something less treacherous?

Many minutes passed and Terra's palms became slippery in the fog. Commanding the magic, she dried them and thought to dry the others' as the fog parted around her and spread upwards, enabling her to see the row of her friends as they made their way down the mountain in single file.

Warlita glanced downward, a smile appearing through the gap between her arms. Terra winked back and took it one step further. Thick fog between her and Sulien, he wouldn't see what she decided to do, commanding the rocks in the mountain to find their feet and made a staircase that started with her and ended with Hank.

Hank could be upset later. What Sulien didn't know wouldn't hurt him, and he was wrong about the magic. It could be molded into anything. Even in the dense fog she had command and was getting more used to how things worked in Marsidia.

In the woods, they hadn't gone any further on foot and had to use the fog to travel. It hadn't made sense that they'd make any headway climbing down the mountain. She used her special vision to see the realm. The fog created interference, making it hard to see anything more than a rudimentary lined map like the ones her mind first saw as she was learning to command magic. It allowed her to see enough and they were making headway. Straight, horizontal lines showed a shelf in the mountain not far below.

The fog suddenly cleared between her and Sulien as her entire foot hit a broad shelf, not the half steps she'd made. As her head fell below the fog blanket, everything cleared, including her vision, and she could see the entire realm. Her jaw fell open in awe.

She stood on a four-foot-wide rock shelf that meandered along the side of the mountain, appearing to narrow in the distance. Her vision clear. No detail hidden from her realm walker sight. The entire valley beneath her radiated colors that spread in horizontal waves, ascending towards the fog shelf and vanishing into it. Tall grasses in the valley flowed like water.

Trees with every color of leaves covered the sides of the circular highlands surrounding the valley beneath. Hues in the sky, some she had no name to describe the shade, vibrated as if alive, pulsing with something beneath the valley. Colors breathed in and out. Water cascaded over the sides of the rocks, dropping into pools and streams reflecting the iridescent colors of the sky. The vibrant purple light she'd seen from above the fog line shone bright like a star. Her curiosity wanted to know what caused it.

The second heartbeat always quietly thumbing inside her beat like a marching band in a parade, matching the symphony of color spreading through the skies from a central point. She didn't think she needed Sulien to find the source but that she could follow her realm walker instinct and it would lead her directly to it. Light radiated from the ground, pulsed with the beat inside her. It was like a beacon pulling her towards it.

In the sky, large horses soared through the air, wide wing spans suspending their bodies countless miles above the earth, their fur bright as the colors of the sky. Sulien hadn't lied. Her instinct wanted to get on one and ride above the valley, glide with it through the sky.

A clatter of falling rocks caught Terra's attention. Furry paws and arms extended from the short sleeves of Mario's shirt.

"I'm ok," he said as his hands returned to normal.

Realm Walker

A gust of strong wind forced him backwards along the rocks. The group braced the wall as their hair was forced backwards over their heads. A Pegasus hung suspended in the air, its large wings pushing the air down as it stared into Mario's eyes.

23

Several suspenseful seconds passed and the Pegasus flashed a glance at Dena than dove downward, resurfacing several feet away.

Dena cleared her throat as everyone except Sulien stared at her, waiting for an explanation. "He meant us no harm. He was merely curious."

"We have a way to walk before we reach the fall that will carry us downward," Sulien said, garnering everyone's attention.

The lightning cords still wound around their chests, they moved in single file along the rock wall of the mountain. Clyde rode in Terra's backpack, his paws on her shoulder, for the journey. The shelf that appeared narrower did get slimmer before they reached the pool of water and the fall.

The group halted as the shelf nearly disappeared a couple feet before the fall. "I can take my plasma and wrap it around that tree," Sulien pointed at a large tree with bright blue leaves, "and we can jump."

Why? Why were they doing things the human way when they were in a land beaming in magic? Terra thought. She could easily extend the shelf and they could safely walk to the fall.

Her thoughts interrupted as Dena said, "Or we can accept help from the Pegasus."

A large gust of wind pushed down on them and nearly drowned out Dena's words as the Pegasus from earlier dropped along the shelf behind Hank, who twirled on his feet in response.

The Pegasus, its golden fur shimmering under the colors of the sky, stood on the ledge. Its wings folded to its side. It was magnificent and larger than any horse Terra had ever seen. She wondered if they were a related species.

Several more Pegasus joined it, their wings flapping in the sky as the one by Hank lowered his front legs and head, motioning for Hank to climb onto its back.

"Climb on," Dena urged. "They are waiting to carry us downward."

The Ring of Betrayal

Hank turned toward Dena then back to the magnificent creature and straddled the rock wall. He paused, flashed Terra a smile, and climbed onto the back of the animal, clutching its mane and lowering himself to its body. It rose with a rush of wind then dropped.

Another Pegasus with a white coat took its spot. Without much hesitation, Mario climbed onto its back. One by one, they climbed onto the backs of the Pegasus. When it was Terra's turn, a silver one dropped onto the ledge, all the colors of the realm mirrored in its coat. It nudged her hand then dropped its front legs. She climbed onto its back. Clyde squirmed downward in her backpack then upwards as the Pegasus took off. By the movement in her backpack, she could tell Clyde was poking his head out of the side as the Pegasus dropped downwards, leaving her stomach on the shelf. She almost squealed in delight like a child on a roller coaster for the first time. It was amazing to be suspended in the air, colors swirling around her, nothing below but valley.

Falls, rock ledges, and trees rushed past them as they plunged several levels. Finally slowing, the Pegasus gently landed on its hooves. Terra leaned down and forward, kissing its head. "Thank you," she whispered into its ear then climbed off.

The silver Pegasus spread its wings as she stepped away and rose into the sky. A royal blue flash caught the corner of Terra's eye as a Pegasus dropped. Sulien's cloak blossoming in front of him with the updraft. She feared they were going to crash then the large animal flapped its wings and lowered them gently to the ground.

Sulien rose up and brought his leg over, dropping onto his feet. He stumbled forward a few steps then fell onto his hands as the animal's large wings brushed against him.

"Seems they don't like you," Warlita jested.

Sulien pulled himself off the ground and dusted golden dirt from his hands. Sparkles lingered in the air as they dropped like feathers. "We can't stay here. We aren't safe," he said, his tone firm.

"Is it the griffons or the manticores? If they're anything like the dangerous Pegasus, I'll take my chances," Kenya huffed.

Hank stuffed his fingers in his front pockets. "We should listen to him. Where do we go that's safe?"

"The griffons are nocturnal predators. They eat small animals." Sulien turned toward Terra and Clyde, who'd climbed onto her shoulder then dove into her backpack. "Their talons and sharp curved beaks can kill you. There is a cave where we can hide for the night. It has a rock face that moves and will shield us from them. It's not far."

Nocturnal? They hadn't seen a change from daylight to night since they'd been in Marsidia but, from Terra's best estimation, yesterday they were above the fog line, below so far was a near different world and maybe night fell.

"How will we know it's night?" Mario asked, mimicking Terra's thoughts.

Sulien's voice grave: "You will know from the screech of the griffons as they rise from their slumber and the blackness that follows. If we move now, we can make it to the cave before that happens."

Alex walked alongside Terra as everyone followed Sulien. "What do you see?" she asked. It was the first time she'd been able to talk with him since they met Sulien.

"Many things, but the most perplexing is you are all surrounded by something. Warlita carries a reflection of whatever is surrounding her, I have flames around myself." He held out his arm. "It looks like fire is eating me." Dropping his arm he continued, "Mario shines like the North Star, Kenya sparkles, Dena is bathed in a golden light, Hank glows with brilliant purple buzzing electricity and you and Sulien are radiant, surrounded in a stream of moving color that pulses with the magic of the realm."

REALM WALKER

His words caught her instantly and they repeated in her mind. She and Sulien carried the same radiant glow and Hank, a warlock, had buzzing electricity. How was that possible? He helped them, and had a plasma cord like Hank. The vision flashed in her mind. She paused, gently grabbing Alex's arm, noting for him to stop. "Do you trust him?"

He shrugged. "I think we have no choice."

In a low voice she nearly whispered, "But we do. I know where the source is."

"He looks like you not Hank, but Hank was raised in Lols, Sulien was raised here surrounded by heavy magic. I would rather have him as a friend than an enemy when we don't know what he is capable of."

Alex was right. It was better to keep one's enemies closer. That's what she'd done with Halsey and it paid off. The Diama of Navarin was a confidante. They walked again, picking up their pace before anyone noticed they'd fallen behind.

Clyde marched beside her on his harness, staying very close. The trees below the fog shimmered brighter than the ones above it. Small flowers shone around the tree trunks,similar to the sarcanthum.

A wail like a cat in heat echoed through the valley. It pierced Terra's ears and she covered them with her palms. The colors of the sky vanished, followed by blackness.

"Hurry," Sulien ordered, his tone anxious.

Her eyes adjusting to the darkness, the glow from the tree and plant leaves the only light. No moon or stars above them. She followed Sulien's voice and rushed ahead with the group, stopping at a rock facing in the mountain.

"Help me," Sulien urged, his palms pressed against the edge of the rock.

Hank thrust his hand toward the rock and it rolled like a wheel, thundering over the ground, revealing a dark cave.

Under his cloak, Terra distinctly saw Sulien's mouth curve into a smile. "You are a true warlock," he said, waving them into the cave.

What did that mean? She thought back to her conversation with Alex. Her thoughts halting as the ground shook behind Terra. She glanced over her shoulder. The glow in the air outlined an animal with a body like a tiger, a mane pouring over its neck, and a curved beak like that of a bird of prey, and feathered wings. It stood so close she felt the heat from its breath on her back.

A hand wrapped around her arm and thrust her forward, but she was halted by the back of her shirt as it caught her in its beak.

24

Lightning flashed on each side of Terra as Hank shot plasma whips at the animal. Undeterred snorts pressed warm air against her back. Dropping Clyde's leash, she ordered, "Go." She watched his long, furry body run into the cave where the others stood and observed. There was enough light from the bioluminescent trees to see the horror written all over their faces. Hank holding onto her arm.

She had this. Wriggling her arm free, she gave Hank a nod with her eyes to confirm she wasn't in any danger. Warm breath curled against her neck as she pushed the energy away from her with a single thought. A hard smack sounded in the air followed by a sliding, crunching sound. When she spun around, the griffon was slumped against a tree.

The animal snorted. She created a bubble around her as flames erupted from the griffon's beak curling, over the bubble. She marched toward the animal and paused.

"Are you hurt?"

Its dark eyes stared into hers and it shook its head as if understanding her words. The flames ceasing, followed by smoke.

Where or why the next line dropped from her mouth she didn't know, but in that moment it seemed important the animal know what she was. "I don't want to hurt you. Go and spread the word that the realm walker is here."

The animal dropped onto all fours, snorted, then turned and raised its feathered wings as it flew into the night.

When she reached the cave, she met grumbles and complaints about how dangerous her actions were.

'You could have been hurt.'

'We could have been hurt.'

'That was foolish.'

It was Sulien who seemed to eye her curiously. She couldn't see his eyes to tell for sure, but his head was turned toward her and his stance was one of pride, with his shoulders squared and his mouth carrying a devious smile. Slivers of memory raced her spine followed by shivers, but she couldn't place the momentary déjà vu. *Who is Sulien?*

"We stay here for the night and continue in the morning," he said, the devious smile playing on his lips vanishing.

She placed a hand on his covered arm. "That was a griffon." He nodded as she continued, "Why does darkness fall when they screech?" It was impossible to see his disapproving glance but she was positive it was there, hidden under his cloak.

"The light you see is caused by the source. When the griffon calls the source goes dark."

He didn't answer her question. Instead of pressing the issue, she rolled the stone behind her closed with a thought and created a light that hung over them like a chandelier. Either she was getting used to being surrounded by magic or it was easier beneath the fog.

Clyde ran in circles around her as she made her way around the chatty group and leaned against the cave wall. It wasn't as smooth as the one above the fog and the crystals were sharper, not worn down.

Dena flashed Terra a glance then turned her eyes away, as if she had something to say but didn't want to announce it in front of the group.

"When will we know it's morning?" Warlita asked, her bangled arms hanging loose at her sides.

"When the crystals in the cave walls shine again," Sulien stated. "There are no dangers in the cave and there is plenty of room further in." He led the way to a jagged entrance and ducked to keep from hitting the rocks as he moved to the other side.

They followed. The crystals didn't glow but sparkled from their glassiness and the light Terra made shining on them. "What is that purple lightning across the ridge?"

Sulien snorted quietly as if disturbed by her question. "It is nothing. A perpetual storm and a dangerous spot to be."

The tone in his voice came with a warning but to Terra it was a dare. He reminded her of someone. She couldn't place who at the moment, but it would come to her eventually.

The cave narrowed and they walked single file. Clyde poked his nose at the wall, reminding her of how he acted when he found the pure soul – her mother. She thought to create a light near him to see better what he was seeing, but thought again. She was becoming more careful and thoughtful with her actions, although her curiosity was fully intact. Later, she would return, sure there was something on the other side of the rocky cave wall.

Realm Walker

The narrow passageway met another rock wall with an even lower rock face. They'd have to crawl to get to the other side unless she used magic. Rethinking, it was probably better not too. She'd used too much already and wasn't convinced Sulien was who he said. The less he knew the better.

On hands and knees, she nearly forced Clyde through as he was intrigued by whatever was on the other side of the cave wall. Once he was through, she followed him. The cavern was large. Massive crystals the size of her hand jutted from the walls in a distinct pattern. Stalagmites and stalactites rose from the ground and fell from the ceiling like a waterfall. In the center of the cavern was a massive hand-carved wheel.

Hank went to it immediately, as if it was a beacon calling to him. She joined him. "What is it?" she asked.

Hank ran a hand over the smooth rock surface, knocking dirt from the top and revealing a part of a dragon's wing. At least a foot in length, embedded into the rock. Its flesh encapsulated in crystal. Terra dusted off the area in front of her, revealing the tip of a pointed ear. She stepped back in shock and horror as Hank continued pushing the dirt from the top, revealing mementos from other realms; a unicorn horn, troll plumage, and a harvester's eye. All surrounded in crystal as if it was resin protecting them.

The Ring of Betrayal

The items Merla requested from each realm when she used them and the seven hybrids to create realm walkers and the veils and curtains between the realms, along with the building of Provence. Missing was the vampire fang and lycan heart. The scrolls. She had Merla's scroll. It was wedged tightly in the pocket of her backpack.

"What is this?!" Hank demanded in anger.

"You may be warlock but you are not of Marsidia," Sulien stated, his words forceful and concise. "This is the place the high wizards met and lived. They watched the realms from this room. It is a place of high importance and only the most righteous of warlocks could enter. Once here they never left until their death."

"Why isn't Drakonia or Canida represented?" Terra asked before thinking. If she'd given it enough thought, she knew the answer already.

Sulien folded his hands together over his abs and calmly stated, "In the beginning there were no lycans or vampires. Something dead cannot live without magic and lycans are born of dragons."

His words didn't match his earlier statement about Canida being one of the realms, nor did they make sense. How would a warlock living his life alone in Marsidia know any of this?

Realm Walker

How does it work?

How did vampires come to be?

Sulien walked around the wheel, his hands cupped behind his back. "It takes five warlocks to activate the wheel in order to see into each of the realms. It hasn't been used in centuries since the warlocks died off. I alone can't activate it."

Terra kept a close watch on him from the corner of her eye.

Kenya joined them at the wheel, always ready for an adventure. "What about six hybrids?"

Sulien paused, releasing his hands to his sides. "That's not why you are here. The wheel is of no use, nor could hybrids activate it…" He paused. "I sense what you're all feeling. You don't trust me. I'm not your enemy but I do need you." He moved his head toward Terra. She felt his eyes burning into her from under his cloak.

Sulien raised his arm, the sleeve of the cloak sliding down it, revealing an arm with semi-healed burns. The flesh in shades of brown and purple. She swallowed hard, attempting to stay calm. "I can't face the source. This is what it did to me, and this…" He pulled the cloak back from the right side of his cheek, the same side as his arm. More deeply burned flesh.

Kenya swallowed hard as she grimaced at the burned, fleshy mess of his cheek. Terra glanced away as it turned her stomach, making what she planned on doing more of a reality. He was the man in her vision. It was the magic between her and Hank that allowed her to see it. Never had she seen Marsidia, but maybe because she'd never tried with Hank's help. Reverting her mind to the present danger, her goal was to face the source. It made the idea of giving her life an appeal and reality that hadn't soaked in until that moment. It was a powerful, sentient blob that didn't approve of everyone. Would it approve of her, or would it maim her as it did him?

Hank twisted on his heel and faced Sulien as he dropped his cloak back over his face. "That explains why you've stayed hidden beneath that cloak, but not what you want from us. I may be a warlock not born of Marsidia, but I grew up with the values, traditions, and tales passed to us from one generation to the next. A warlock would know better than to face the source. No warlock has ever attempted it. We are guardians of it, protectors, not takers. You are no warlock."

Sulien's lips curled into a devious smile. "And your adventure stops here."

An invisible force dragged Hank backwards. He reached for the wheel, but even his long arms were too far away for him to grasp the side. Terra lunged for him but was blocked by another invisible force. One by one all her friends, and even Clyde, were dragged unwillingly into a side cavern.

A rock face built up around the entrance. Terra fought and pushed against the force surrounding her. She took her finger to slice it like jelly and reach the other side but it immediately came back together no matter what she tried. She even portalled herself to the other side of the room but it went with her. She was stuck and her friends were locked away, separated from her. With all the power she had Sulien, was stronger.

Sulien faced her. "You're the only one I need. You will face the source for me and channel its energy into me." He dropped the hood from his head. His shining hair the color of the light she'd made. His eyes dazzled in various colors and recognition coalesced within her, all the links falling into place. His shifty smile and gaze, one of distrust. Kelon, the man who she woke up to in Aradia after she fainted when the sky sizzled in lightning that ripped the veils apart.

Her eyes dropping to his out of place blue tennis shoes. It was Terina who saw them and the creature wearing them transform, and Gwond… He often wore blue tennis shoes. She gulped as her eyes rose to face the man with hair like hers. Cyrus.

25

Terra gasped. Her breathing sped and she balled her fists. Energy crackled inside her, anger resounded. As she unballed her fists, the invisible barrier surrounding her dissolved away. "I will not!"

Her mission was to save life, not collect the power for herself or anyone else. She carried the grimoire to reverse the spell. Power she didn't even want and, come hell or high water, she wasn't giving it to him.

Calmly, he stared deep into her eyes. "You will. Without the warlock I'm stronger than you. You will do as I ask."

She folded her arms over her chest in defiance. "Is this the father-daughter moment you waited for? Our first meeting. What have you become? You went from realm walker freedom fighter to…to…" and then the words lodged in her throat came forward as the picture became clearer, "vile one."

His nose twitched and his eyes narrowed. "Go!" he ordered, pointing towards another cavern.

Fuming, she sucked in a deep breath and marched forward. She'd find a way to escape and release her friends, but she did need to face the source. That was the purpose of her mission. She'd go along with him. Using the thick magic of the realm, she searched for her connections to Clyde and Hank. Unable to feel, them she felt alone.

The cavern led to carved rock steps that led down. "M'ra had faith in you. She believed in you, saw the good in you."

"M'ra sold her soul to rule Drakonia. The ache for power and control runs through our veins."

"You think I have that hunger. That's why you believe I'll use the source to channel its magic. What if I choose to keep it for myself, or what if it reads my intentions and does to me what it did to you?"

"You won't. You don't want the power, but you like being powerful. That's why you've only broken the surface of what you can do. Your mother was like you. She enjoyed what she could do but refused to use it to save her own life. She left you motherless and hid you away from me. You can move mountains, shape worlds, define borders, yet you believe in saving this wretched world that hates what they created. Life will wither and new life, a different kind of life, will flourish. One that follows my command."

He thought he'd rule a new world, one he designed. Hate boiled and simmered inside her. He was right. She didn't want the power. It was her goal to give it back to the source. Instead of going down his dark path, she thought to find the goodness in him if any was left. "Tell me what happened. Help me understand."

"Our conversation is over. Silence."

The carved rock stairway wound round and round as they went further and further into the mountain.

Hank

The rune on his leg ached with Terra's departure. It was a connection between them. Desperate, he created sound waves to shake the rock wall loose and free them. The waves had little effect as they moved beneath the rock wall that held steady. He forced lightning at it in a rage. It sizzled and the rocks sparked before fizzling out.

Alex put a hand on Hank's. "Your magic will not free us. Save your energy."

Hank turned to face Alex who stared, as always, into what appeared to be nothingness. A void of sorts. "Then what do we do? He has Terra. I should have known from the start he wasn't a warlock."

"Then we all should have known. What's done is done. Sit with us. Let's collect our thoughts. Everything that's happened was meant to happen and we are all here for a purpose. Nothing is coincidence," Alex said in a calm, collected voice, moving to the middle of the cavern where everyone sat in a circle, Clyde sniffing along the walls.

Hank joined the circle, as did Alex, but found it difficult to sit still as his foot tapped nervously beneath his leg.

Dena folded her hands in front of her and addressed the group. "The griffons are under the control of something dark. She didn't want to harm Terra but is losing herself to the darkness. They are becoming shells, slaves to something evil. It's becoming harder to fight it off. That's why the darkness falls when they call. I wasn't able to get more and what I got came in pieces."

"How do we save Terra?" Hank couldn't help but worry for her. His connection to her stronger than ever as the rune ached to find her, to be at her side. He was her guardian and needed desperately to be with her.

"We don't," Kenya snorted. "She has her own demons to battle. If we went to the source with her, what use would we be?"

"I've been fighting the shift since I arrived. I thought it was the thick magic, but I'm beginning to think it's something else. We're hybrids with unique skills. In my bobcat form I'm connected to other animals. I'm a predator, a hunter. My senses allow me to note the smallest vibrations and changes in sound. I can see further…" Mario admitted as he addressed the group.

Warlita pushed a strand of hair behind her ear, bangles clinking against her arm. "I can find Terra." She held her arm up. "I gave you each a bracelet." She turned her head and glanced at Clyde. "Something's got at him. He hasn't left the walls."

Hank stood. Moving to the wall, he studied it. "A door?" Clyde stood on his hind legs and pressed his front paws against Hank's leg. "What?" he asked the ferret, as if it would respond.

Dena leaned down, offering a hand to the ferret who pressed his front paws against her palm. "Talk to me?"

The ferret dropped onto all fours and ran back to the wall, pressing his face against a crystal.

Taking a step away from the wall, Hank studied the crystals then spun on his heel and studied the patterns of crystals in the other walls. He whipped his head back to the wall and pointed. "These crystals aren't random. Look at the others - there's no pattern - but these are spaced equally apart."

Warlita brushed against Hank as she stepped in front of him. She pressed her hand against one and it buzzed, lighting for a moment. She grabbed another and it did the same. "I can figure this out." Pressing one after another the wall shook but didn't budge. "It's a matter of hitting the right pattern."

The rune ached. Hank clutched it, quickly moving his hand away as fire scorched against his palm. He shook his hand as a reaction then studied his palm. There were no marks.

His actions caught Kenya's attention. She touched his pants. "What is that?" she asked.

He knocked her hand away. The rune burned through his pants, its outline marked in his jeans. "My connection to Terra. I have to find her," he said, his voice frantic.

"I got it!" Warlita hollered, bringing everyone's attention back to her as the wall shook and crumbled.

A teal light flashed behind them and Hank spun on his heel to face a vampire. His dark hair slicked back, dressed in designer jeans and finely threaded polo shirt. He knew him as the vampire that M'ra secured to follow Terra. He opened his mouth to speak when, from the corner of his eye, he noted the floor appeared to move beneath his feet.

Taking his attention from the vampire known as Bane, he glanced down as ferrets flooded the room.

26

The never-ending staircase sank into darkness at each corner until her light caught up illuminating more steps winding further downhill into darkness. Terra paused, pushing her back against the stone wall. "I need a rest and food."

"There's no time. Move."

She slid down, parking herself on a step, her eyes dropping to the floor. "No! I need food."

"Fine. You must have something in that backpack."

She pulled it over her shoulder and reached in, pulling out a bag of beef jerky. "Are you hungry?"

When he didn't respond, she pushed at his buttons. "If you're so powerful, why are we walking down these steps instead of portalling? Wouldn't that be easier?" She thought of the ascendant in her bag.

His foot pushed against her leg. "Break is over. Move."

She stood, adjusted her backpack, then glanced over her shoulder and bated him. "You really can't make me do things can you?"

"You have done plenty that I asked, everything that I asked. Every challenge put before you, every test. But you never pieced the clues together."

He'd been hiding in plain sight, using her, gaining her trust. M'ra, as a hybrid, hid herself and her family in Verboten as trolls as she could shift anyone into a troll. Was it easier for Cyrus too? As Kelon, an elf, his form wasn't as solid. It shifted, further creeping Terra out. Betrayal dropped her heart to the stone floor. She liked Gwond as an instructor. She stopped and turned to face him.

"Gwond. You hid all these years as a troll waiting for what? Me? Every mystery you clued me into like a good little soldier. I found everything. But it's all meaningless. The antiquities room. You wanted me to figure out who you were. It wasn't to understand who I was. It was to finally have someone see you for yourself." The words rolled off her tongue.

"Only my daughter could find those things, could go to every realm, unlock Merla's cave, wake up magic where it was otherwise dead. Your mother hid you away from me as if she had to protect you from me, your own father. I could have taught you so much. We could have lived in a world I built for the two of us until you were old enough." His voice boomed in anger.

Crazy talk. The man was certifiable, but there was something to his words that had bothered Terra since finding the book in Merla's cave that led to the grimoire. Her fae friends couldn't unlock the hidden cavern, only she could. "Merla's cave was part of the spell and only a realm walker could enter. You used me, betrayed my trust. You are not the father I needed or any father to me," she spat, her words loaded with hate.

"Blood of my blood, haven't you learned anything about level 4 magic? You will make my transformation complete!"

Transformation? Into what? Dare she ask? His scarred face filled with loathing and a hint of jealousy in his hazel eyes. She recognized the green monster. It ate her up in Verboten when all the girls swarmed over Hank. Cyrus had no ambitions to take her to the source but to sacrifice her, giving him the connection to the source she held. Level 4 magic used sacrifice and she was his. Whatever he planned on transforming into he needed her. Blood of his blood.

As she did with Rosette, her gaze into his eyes was unwavering. When her mother finally went to Tranquility she'd felt her warm, loving energy coalesce inside her. All the realm walkers who died, it was she who gained their strength. It hadn't returned to the source just as her mother's hadn't. It went into the innocent, unknowing child she'd been. Her eyes were open now. All of it came together as shadows moved over the walls and the ceiling blocking out her light. Cyrus was the vile one and leader of the Council of Divination. They'd fed on his suffering. He'd fed on theirs. This new life was death. Fractured souls whom he felt he could lead. They'd promised him the power he hungered and ached for. The new life would be his death and they would rule the realms.

Their coldness brushed against her skin as she shuddered. What happened that made someone willing to sacrifice their own flesh and blood? Was there any of him left as he succumbed to the darkness? The shadow energy strong. They hated him, used him. "You misunderstand them. They are dark souls who want to destroy you," she pleaded with him.

"It is you who doesn't understand. Your power will rest in me and the source will be mine to control. I will build a world, bringing life out of death. An improvement on the necromancer's failed attempt. I have seen. I bear the scars from when the source failed to destroy me."

Necromancer? She pushed the thought away as unimportant in the moment. The shadows swirling around her, their thoughts and intentions whispering in the air.

With a thought, she pushed against them, forcing them against the wall and ceiling. "They will destroy you. They hate what we are. I came here to save life, not destroy it —" Her words were interrupted by a teal flash. Hank at her side as quickly as Bane clutched Cyrus' arms, holding them behind his back.

"Do what you must do. Quickly."

Hank clutched her hand, her mind reeling. Unable to ask the questions firing off in rapid succession in her mind.

Warlita stepped out from behind Bane and brushed past a stunned Terra. "This way." She waved her arm forward down the winding corridor of steps.

She gave one last glance at Cyrus as Hank tugged her along. He struggled against Bane's powerful grasp. Terra let go of the force holding back the shadows. They swirled and coiled inside Cyrus. Bane winked at her then he and Cyrus vanished in a teal flash.

27

Her first thought centered not on Bane and how he was there or how they got free, but immediately moved to her ferret. He was a piece of her. "Where is Clyde?"

"They're fine. Their job is something different," Hank responded, referring to the whole group, not only Clyde. "Mario can shift, Dena can communicate with animals, Kenya can weave spells, and Alex sees things others don't."

Warlita, in her cheetah boots, clomped down the stairs. "Clyde is more a part of this realm than any of us. He and the other ferrets are leading them."

Other ferrets? "What will happen to Bane?"

Hank chuckled, easing Terra's tensions a little. "He's a vampire in a place with no sunlight, he'll be fine."

"He's giving us the head start we need," Warlita responded. "We don't have much time."

Questions rapid-fired in Terra's brain. "How did he get here?"

"Enough with the questions. We're here!" Warlita pressed her hands against various crystals embedded in the cave wall. It dissolved in front of their eyes.

What happened in the time they were separated? "I don't understand."

"You will," Warlita croaked with irritation. "We have to utilize the window of time Bane's given us."

Hank stepped to the other side of the wall, his hand tightly clutched around Terra's as he pulled her in. Warlita following behind. The wall came together and crystals reformed.

The area was small and stuffy, barely big enough for the three of them. "Hold on," Warlita said as she pressed her palms against the crystals. They flashed in a type of code. The floor beneath them rumbled and a lightning cord wrapped around her, pulling her close to Hank. The floor dropped beneath their feet, leaving their stomachs behind as they shot downward. The elevator-type thing slowed and stopped. The lightning cord snaked away from her and coiled into Hank. Terra took a step away from Hank. Warlita stood no more than a foot away from her. Terra folded her arms over her chest. "Before you open that door and we go any further I need to know what's going on."

Warlita stepped forward. "There isn't time. If we don't use this window we may not see tomorrow. Cyrus is powerful. Those things are wraiths. They feed on darkness, hate, and revenge. Their power is growing. Cyrus is their vessel."

"The rune is finished," Hank said, turning his leg toward Terra. Burned into his jeans was the rune. She recognized part of it. The rest was new. "It's a source rune."

How did he did he know that? That didn't help Terra make any more sense of what was happening. The only thing that made any sense was Cyrus being the vessel of the wraiths. She'd seen the dark shadows swirl around them. She'd held them back and, when she let go, they coiled inside him. Otherwise, she was more confused. The urgency in Hank's tone and Warlita's irritated stance, she understood they needed to move now.

Terra nodded and Warlita pressed against the crystals. The rocks disappeared and a steady hum vibrated inside her as she stepped into a large cavern. A soft, colorful glow emanated from the other end. The source.

Kenya

This was the end of the line for the ferrets. The leaves of the trees shed some light on the mountain side but they were sparser here than on the other side of the mountain. Kenya swallowed as she put on her brave exterior and stepped out of the cave.

A tug at her leg nearly made her jump. She peered down at Clyde who stood on his hind legs. "What are you doing here? Get back in the cave," she whispered to him. He moved between her legs followed by a creamier-colored ferret without the mask or dark-tipped ears. "Both of you." She stepped forward and they followed. "Fine," she mumbled.

"Shh…" Dena said, putting a finger to her mouth as she grimaced at Kenya.

Who died and made her my mom? Kenya thought as she lowered her backpack. The ferrets scrambled inside it and she lifted it up, carefully hoisting it over her back. *I never realized how heavy you are. How does Terra do it?*

As if one of them heard her thoughts, a needlelike claw poked at her back. She pushed her chest out in response then shifted her gaze to Dena who hadn't seemed to notice. Kenya didn't need to be reminded they were still in griffon territory and would be until they crossed the rock wall and made it uphill to the fallen tree which marked the village of the same name.

It was Cyrus who used wraiths to inhabit the griffons and trap the warlocks on the mountain, according to the ferrets, and they were to save them. She wasn't sure about the hero stuff now that she was actually doing it. Quietly, they moved toward the rock wall. She hated heights, not that she'd let on. So far she'd avoided looking down and she wasn't going to start now. Keeping her head high, she followed behind Dena who walked in Mario's bobcat footsteps.

Once he'd given in to the shift, he was able to communicate with the ferrets and Dena. The ferrets hadn't been trapped; they'd hidden, terrified of what the griffons had turned into. Mario paused and Kenya's heart raced. What was it? She hoped they didn't run into any fire-breathing, wraith-inhabited griffons. When he continued, her heart slowed and she sucked in a deep breath.

They reached the rock face. It was several feet long and no more than two feet wide. She quickly took her eyes away to avoid the depths below. *You can do this. You can do this.*

So as not to squish the ferrets and avoid accidentally looking down, she faced the rock wall and dug her hands into the rough surface. She wouldn't see any griffons either. That was something she did want to see. It was too late to change her mind as Alex scooted his back along the rock face behind her. He was lucky, as he couldn't see down.

Her tough exterior was slowly melting away as she scooted along the rock face. A stone fell in front of her eyes. It clunked as it hit the ledge. She glanced upwards. A beaked shadow stood directly above her. Its talons curled over the side of the rock wall. She tapped Dena, getting her attention, and pushed her pointer finger upwards. Dena tilted her head and covered her mouth. She found Alex's hand and pointed a finger upwards against it. He got the message and the three of them stood very still.

She couldn't see Mario, as Dena blocked her view. With his keen senses he should have picked up on it before anyone else. Why hadn't he said anything? Of course, he didn't want to freak them out. Well, she was freaked. The griffon hadn't seemed to notice them. Her heart raced and sounded in her ears like the Daytona 500. If she lived through this, if they lived through this, she was going to clutch the flat lands of Provence for a week.

A few rocks slid along the wall in front of her, one hitting her nose. She squeezed her eyes shut to absorb the pain instead of screaming. Air rushed against her back as large wings spread into the sky.

Within moments, they were on dirt again and the land moved upwards with a gentle slope. She followed Mario and Dena into a cluster of trees that offered some camouflage and nearly hugged one as she was so happy to be off the rock face. At least here she could use her magic more readily. When they reached the end of the tree cluster, Mario paused. He glanced over his shoulder at Dena then took off running.

The sound of wings flapped into the air and Dena pointed uphill as she ran into the open and upwards, towards another cluster of trees. The griffon soared through the air as it followed Mario. His legs quick and agile, he dodged its talons as she lost sight of him running into a large fallen tree.

She wished Dena or Mario had some way of telepathically communicating with her instead of sudden decisions and movements. She and Alex sprinted after Dena and made it to the cluster of trees and through them. There were buildings. Similar to the village they rode the fog to, only more. One by one, they went around the back of a building and peeked around the side before cutting across to the next and the next.

A snort and rustle of dirt sounded from the other side of the building. The ferrets wriggled in Kenya's backpack. She glanced at their surroundings. There was another building across and to the right; beyond that, woods. According to the ferrets, once they made it uphill to the other side of the woods they'd be out of griffon territory. She needed something to distract the griffon. A medium-sized rock caught her eye. *Perfect!*

"Lift," she whispered. The rock shook then rose from the ground. It was larger than she thought as the buried part rose from the ground. "Up," she commanded it. Levitation was one of her newer skills and she'd aced it. Once the rock was higher than the roof and dangling in the air she commanded it, "Sling."

It flew over the rooftop like a rocket and crashed into what sounded like a building and thudded to the ground. "Run."

She grasped Alex's hand and pulled him forward as she sprinted across dirt, behind the building, and up the hill, letting go of Alex's hand. She glanced over her shoulder and stopped in horror. Dena stumbled backwards towards the trees. A griffon grunting and snorting as it moved closer to her.

No, no, no! She turned her head, searching for something to distract it, when it came to her. The trees. "I'm sorry I have to do this to you." She pressed her hand against a tall tree. "Snap and fall." Its base cracked, echoing across the mountain, and dropped forward. The griffon tilted its panther-like head upwards and breathed fire into the air as Dena rolled out of the way and scrambled to her feet.

Leaves burned and curled as the wood scorched but didn't fully burn, landing with a thwack on the griffon's head. Kenya scrambled down the hill and caught Dena's hand, helping her up the hill.

Without glancing over her shoulder at the tree, she continued running toward the buzzing purple light now clearly in their vision.

28

Terra stepped back as a monstrous beast with the head of a lion and the body of a man stepped through the cave entrance, blocking her from the soft glow of the source. A dark brown mane flowed over its shoulders. A lion's tail swung behind its legs. Its mouth opened, showing large, sharp, predator teeth as it growled into the air, echoing off the walls and ringing in Terra's ears. A wraith-possessed manticore, she assumed.

It was the size of a giant, standing in her estimate eight feet, maybe nine. She didn't have a growl or a deadly bite but she had Hank and whatever the source rune was. "Go back, Warlita," she ordered, her eye on the manticore as she blasted a ball of energy at it, hitting it square in the chest. It growled, but not in pain.

She stepped to the side. Its eyes followed her. An electric whip caught its neck but it gripped a hand around it, flinging it off. Hank stumbled before regaining his composure and sending double lightning whips against its side. Terra stomped the floor, causing a wave of rocks to crash beneath its feet. It stumbled but didn't fall.

"Stronger together," Hank said as he sent a ball of light towards Terra. She smiled as she absorbed its energy. Like Sier, their practice. She pushed the energy downward as he flooded her with light. The ground shook in waves that lifted the rocky floor a few feet off the ground. The manticore teetered before dropping to all fours.

The manticore swung a large arm and hand the size of her head toward her. She ducked and rolled away. When she got back onto all fours, Hank had formed two sizzling lightning swords.

He wielded them like a pro, their light dazzling the manticore, its black eyes fixed on them. Hank thrust one into its side. Its mouth lifted, the skin wrinkling beneath its nose as it bared its teeth. Another sword already formed in Hank's hand.

Realm Walker

The manticore lifted a large hand to swat him away. Hank spun and lopped it off. The hand dropping to the floor, acid spilled from it, burning the ground where it fell. "The source rune doesn't allow me to face the source, but to kill the beast who tries to stop you. You must go," Hank said, recognizing from his various tones that his words didn't relay the whole truth. He moved closer to the manticore and thrust a lightning blade towards it. It growled in agony and annoyance. A forked tongue, like that of a snake, spilled from its mouth, whipping toward Hank as it slinked nearer to him.

Hank spun again, avoiding its tongue, his braids flailing into the air. She thought it was the most sexy thing she'd seen as she moved towards the doorway. Taking one last glance as Hank dropped to the ground and slid beneath the manticore, pushing a lightning blade through its chest. It howled in pain as she entered the cavern.

It was empty and led to another cavern. The light beaming in various colors, its hum a call to her. She ran across the empty cavern towards an arch. Once through it, she paused and marveled. The light shining in brilliant colors from a large blob in the center of the room, much like the blob in the dungeon. Dangling above it wasn't stars but shriveling roots. They formed the symbols on Hank's rune. Serenity Tree.

The Ring of Betrayal

Come closer dear one, hummed through the air.

Cautiously, Terra stepped toward the blob, its sentient warmth enveloping her. "I've come to give you back what was stolen and to save the life of Serenity Tree and all life."

You can't give back what is given freely but you must take what was stolen, the air hummed.

"I don't understand." Too often had those words crossed her mind.

You will. Come to me and I will show you.

Terra stepped closer and the blob rose up around her like liquid, blanketing her inside a cocoon.

Images flashed around her. Seven spheres hurtled through darkness from every angle, towards a single sphere that radiated many colors. Shades of pink, greens and blues, gold and silver, left the small sphere. It was breathtaking until each sphere smashed into the center one. Debris flew away and fused, forming a layer over the jumble. The rainbow of lights no longer radiated and everything went dark.

Hank hypothesized correctly. The carvings and images in the dungeon were remnants, echoes of the past. The collision of the realms and the forming of Lols.

It was a tragedy when the realms collided, but life found a way. The few survivors, here in Marsay. It became known as the inner realm of Marsidia. There were very few survivors in the middle realms. Most perished except the elvarin, the dryads, and nymphs. Warlocks moved into the realm and became known as realm walkers, simply meaning they walked among the settled dust of the realms. A seed of the Serenity Tree flourished and carried magic into the middle realms. New life formed, while the survivors were nomadic, eventually settling into various lands and developing certain skills, eventually breaking away into dragons, fae, elves, trolls, and harvesters. There was always trouble in the middle realms and so some moved further into the outer realm assuming they would live by their rules, dictate their own lives, but the outer realm already had life, inhabitants – humans.

The humans were impressed with their abilities and forced them to create tools so they too could harness magic. The magic ones moved further and further north to escape the humans, some stayed, assimilating, as they weren't pureblooded, finding ways to hide their magic. By this time so many generations had passed they didn't know of the middle realms anymore or where their magic came from, only that it was forbidden.

It was the fae who found a portal to the middle realms beneath the ice. It was the warlocks who helped others cross into the middle realms. When the humans learned what was happening, they came after them with blades and axes. The humans were so large in number even magic couldn't fend them all off, and so warlocks and other magical beings were left behind to protect the magic of the middle and inner realms from those who worshipped it, who envied what it could get them.

The fae and warlock alike wrote the spell that sealed the veil between the outer realm, now known as Lols, from the other realms. It was nearly the same spell that created you. The fae are descendents of the warlocks. The elves descendants of the elvarin and fae. Trolls descended from warlocks and dryads. Magic affected each realm differently. Other realms had completely new life, such as the harvesters and dragons.

Images of the frozen highlands of Sier flashed over the blob, followed by violent eruptions of lava from the other side of the highlands, differentiating the ice and fire dragons. Lava flows covered the land that is now Canida, which somehow allowed the lycans to evolve. *The vampires were a product of the great warlock necromancer, Drakal.* Terra suddenly understood Cyrus' words about the necromancer. He wanted to be more powerful than him and envisioned a superior species, but it was all smoke and mirrors, as the wraiths loathed him and planned to betray him.

It wasn't many generations later when the warlocks became suspicious of those from Lols. The land of lost souls. They'd been away too long and had acquired too much humanity and greed, so Hovrath made the keys that closed off Marsidia from the other realms.

Realm Walker

This wasn't done to protect me. It was done to limit the magic accessible to the middle realms. It was at this point warlocks defined themselves as the guardians of the source, but they realized Serenity Tree needed a clear path to the magic that allowed its seed to continue life and so Hovrath exited Marsidia, never to return, as he carefully planted the enter stones in the lavender seas. He hid the exit stones, covering their magic trail with a disguise enchantment. The troll hybrid found them, but had no power to break the enchantment. You, as a realm walker, designed of a similar concoction of the spell carries the energy that dissolved the enchantment, only you didn't understand. Your father did. He stole those stones and waited for you to reveal the other stones to him.

Merla was more than a powerful fae, she was a historian. That's how she knew of the spell and was able to replicate it to create the veils and curtains between the realms and realm walkers who were to keep the peace.

Humans had no power. That's why they were called commoners and the land of lost souls was chosen, as it fit because those who lost their way ended up there.

You come here wanting to save lives and give up the control of magic handed to you. Now that you have seen the bloody, backstabbing history of it all, do you still want to preserve life?

Inside the cocoon of the source, Terra's thoughts flowed. *Yes, not all life is bad.* As the source had shown her the sordid history of the realms and beings, she showed the source her life with her father and Noah, her friends in Provence. Her friends here who followed her into danger because they believed they were doing the right thing.

Then so be it, but you must do two things first in order for that to be. First, you must stop fighting your feelings for Hank. You are eclipsed souls. It is time you embraced that.

Eclipsed souls. What is that? Terra inquired.

The source chuckled, its blobbiness wiggling like jelly with Terra inside. *You were chosen because you are pure and not because of your virginity.* It wiggled more at its own joke. *You chose him as your partner when you kissed him that day. Why do you fight him?* Terra hadn't chosen him on a conscious level. Had she seen into his heart that moment when they attempted to combine their magic? *Your hearts are good and you will not succumb to the great power bestowed on you, but I can't simply grant you the power. You must take it.*

No, Terra didn't want it. She came here to return it. *But what if I choose not to?*

Then you will perish and the realms will crumble, as Cyrus will use magic bestowed on him to destroy and the darkness growing inside him to obliterate. You see, I am magic, but can't control what others do with that magic. When magic is sealed with a blood sacrifice, that is a pact and the only way to undo it is through blood. Blood for blood or blood of blood.

Remembering what the Serenity Tree said, Terra asked, *Then life will start anew?*

Yes. The tree is dying because of hate, strife, war, and greed. The causes of each veil and curtain robbed Serenity of what she needs to survive. From her seed will grow new life and the cycle will start again. The tree flashed over the blobby, jelly sides of the source. It was mighty. Its trunk as wide as a home, taller than a skyscraper, and its branches covering nearly half of Aradia. The tree Terra met was only a fraction of that. It hurt her heart.

It seems you have much to think about.

Too much. Her mind couldn't process everything but she did have one more question. *Hank has a source rune. That makes him and I eclipsed souls. Can he stand before you as I can?*

Yes. Magic can't be taken or given without blood and I am only the source of magic but I can give runes which allow magical abilities. The source rune binds him to you and me and your father, Cyrus. Together you have the tools to destroy who he's become. You lack the time to think this over. Make your decision.

The blob left Terra as it lowered itself and molded back into a ball-like sphere. It seemed there wasn't much of a choice. Either she let everything perish or saved what was left of life to mold it into something better.

When she entered the next cavern, sizzles of blue light mingled with the colors of the source and the clanking of metal filled her ears. Rushing into the cavern where she left Hank, another manticore swung its large hand at Hank while Warlita swung an axe into its side.

In her fishnet tights, cheetah print combat boots, and black skirt, an axe in one hand and metal shield in the other, she looked like a dystopian warrior princess.

Hank wound a lightning cord around the weakened, acid-bleeding manticore's neck and pulled it to the ground. Warlita, axe in hand, brought it down on the manticore's head. It cut through the flesh. The manticore convulsed and stopped.

Hank brought in the lightning whip and dropped his hands to his knees while Warlita lowered her axe and shield and sucked in a deep breath.

The first manticore lay where Hank felled it. A second was an acidic mess several feet away, and the third lay where they left it. Hank raised his head, taking her in as if he and Warlita hadn't been noble, war-scarred warriors, he asked, "What did it say?"

She took his hands in hers. "It said to stop fighting you. The source rune ties us together." Terra knew there wasn't really a choice or a decision to make. "We have to work as a team, trust each other, and take what Cyrus stole. Blood of blood."

In that tender moment, as she looked deeply into his dark eyes, she forgot about the slayed manticores and all the havoc around her.

"Stronger together," Hank replied, raising a hand to her cheek.

"Stronger together," she repeated, tilting her head upwards, awaiting the touch of his soft lips.

"We don't have time for that," Warlita urged as she moved closer to them, her axe raised and shield up.

Terra shifted her eyes away from Hank who turned his head and stared at the archway of the cavern. Cyrus filled the small space.

29

The buzzing purple light seemed much closer than it truly was, but the Pegasus came through for them again, dropping them off outside the cave. Kenya looked to the sky as the magnificent creatures flew away, until she could see them no more.

Carefully, she took the pack off her back and let the ferrets out. They took off running, chasing each other and rolling in the grass, to stand back and sniff at each other. "Looks like you found a friend. What's your name?" Kenya asked.

Cora. Kenya stepped back in shock as the thought rolled into her head. "Cora," she repeated. "Are your people in there? Can you help us free them?"

They aren't my people. The magic of the land will open it on your command. "That telepathic connection is real." All this time she'd thought Terra was full of it.

The ferret didn't respond, as the relationship seemed to take a more serious turn. "You found yourself a Jill. Good work, Clyde."

A chuckle erupted beside her. "Are you having a conversation with the animals?" Alex asked between laughs.

Kenya retorted, feeling a bit silly for having a conversation with a ferret, "I was. She talks, into my head."

"You sure you weren't just imagining it?"

"No! What Dena and Mario are the only ones allowed to talk to animals? What about Terra? She talks to Clyde all the time," she said, becoming defensive.

Dena joined them. "We have bigger problems than who can have conversations with ferrets. If we split up and walk around the mountain, maybe we can find a way in."

"Yes, Mom." Kenya snorted, rolling her eyes.

Dena huffed and shook her head in frustration.

Kenya and Alex took one side, while Dena and Mario took the other. Mario had escaped the griffon and made it to high ground, meeting up with them soon after Kenya felled the tree. "The ferret really spoke to you. What did it say?"

"She," Kenya clarified, "told me her name and a rhyme when I asked how to free the warlocks."

"She told you how to free them? So why are we walking around the mountain?!"

It was the first time she'd ever heard Alex raise his voice. "Mother Dena, who thinks she knows best." Her toned filled with sarcasm.

Alex ran a hand through his hair. "OK. We're all tired, we haven't eaten. It's been a long day. What did she say?"

"The magic of the land will open it on your command."

Alex chuckled again, "Of course! That's how everything works here. We think it and it happens."

Kenya imagined the mountain dissolving around the warlocks and them running out, happy to be free. Alex was right, she needed sleep and food. Nothing happened and she placed a hand on her hip. "That didn't work."

"There're four of us."

Midway around the mound, the four came together. Alex explained they should combine and request the warlocks to be free.

Dena shrugged. "Makes sense. Why didn't we already think of that?"

Because you're a bossy b… Kenya collected her thoughts that should be focused on other things.

Mario, no longer in his bobcat form but human form, took her hand. Alex took her other hand and Kenya took his. Together, they stood as a team and requested the mound dissolve and free the warlocks.

As if the mound was made of dust, it blew away layer by layer, revealing a crater in the ground and hundreds of warlocks; children, adults, teenagers. Kenya's mouth dropped immediately and she knelt, reaching out a hand. A man closest to her picked up a child clinging to his legs and held her up. Kenya put both arms around the child and, with a touch of levitation, brought the child out of the pit.

The others followed and helped the warlocks out of the pit, a combination of human skill and magic.

Once they were all free a group of three, the warlock council, introduced themselves. Their everyday clothing didn't set them apart from anyone else. Two were females and the other a male.

The female with braids wrapping her head like a crown introduced herself as Nema. "We appreciate your sacrifice to free us from the captivity of the vile one; keeper of the wraiths."

They further explained how he'd used the Stones of Hovrath – stones that were lost centuries ago - to enter. They have a special portal into the land. Darkness swallowed the light, as wraiths were the first to come through the portal, immediately inhabiting the griffons and manticores. As the vile one came through, other wraiths attached to him like a magnet. Their power, fed by hate and rage, combined with his connection to the source, the warlocks couldn't fend them off. They didn't have enough power between them to fight such a massive army.

"We weren't prepared," said the male in a soft voice. "We are peaceful and live as one with the source. It provides for all our needs. We have become complacent. Now we must gather and fight the evil, drive it from our land."

"How do we fight it?" Kenya asked. It was a commonsense question.

"We use our sunlight runes to devour the wraiths."

Why hadn't they already done that? These warlocks were a few cards shy of a full deck. "Can we amplify your light?"

Mena smiled. "Inside every cave are crystals. They amplify the source which gives us runes. Through those crystals we can spread light into every corner of Marsidia."

That was great, but would the light kill them, send them back through the portal, or into Cyrus? Now that she thought about it, the whole rescue of the warlocks was anticlimactic. Sure, they were happy to get out of the crater, but something didn't sit right with her. "You haven't asked us why we're here. You weren't surprised to see us. Why is that?"

The soft-voiced male looked to his counterparts, who gave him a nod of approval. "Runes. Among us we have many runes. Some have the ability to see into the future, the past, and the present. We knew what was coming. We are only tools in the battle. The warlock you came with has a source rune and the other, the female, she is a conduit of the source. They must find a way within themselves, as a team, to destroy the vile one. We can only assist in the war."

Kenya glanced to Alex, who also had the ability to *see*. Was he warlock? He was dragon which gave him his special vision but was he warlock too?

It was Dena who asked, "What is our part?"

Mena smiled. "Even the seers don't know the final outcome, only possibilities."

That really didn't answer Dena's question. Kenya didn't have patience on a regular non-stressful day. Her patience was dangling by a string. "That's not what she asked."

The third warlock, who hadn't yet spoken, replied, "We don't know everyone's part, but we do know we must all use our magic and the magic of the land to assist your friends. Our daylight runes, amplified by the source, can rid the land of the wraiths."

In the mood to argue, Kenya gritted her teeth behind her lips, noting the pleading expression on Dena, Alex, and Mario's faces. She remembered what Hank said when they first got there. It wasn't their realm. They were foreigners and should be respectful of the warlocks. Still gritting her teeth, she forced a smile.

"Is there anything we can do now to help your people?" Mario asked.

"Yes, you can rest. You did your job, let us do ours," Mena answered.

Kenya wasn't going to argue that one.

30

A teal light flashed between Cyrus and Terra. As the light dissolved, Bane stood between them, his clothes ripped, shirt hanging from his back, bruises covering his exposed flesh, his left arm dangling at an odd angle. He lunged for Cyrus who flung him over his head into the cavern behind him, his body landing with a thud.

Terra shook her head in disgust, the crystals in the wall grabbing her attention. Some were sharp as daggers. Using the energy of the room, she pulled them forward out of the wall in the cavern where Bane lay and shot them all towards Cyrus.

They showered around him, but not a single one hit him, as he pushed them to the ground. "The source allowed you in," he growled. Shadows swirled around him as his anger flared.

"It did."

"What did it tell you?"

"It told me there's good inside you but I must rid the evil first," she 100% lied as she attempted to appeal to anything good that might be inside him.

He growled. This side of him was nothing like the helpful troll instructor, Gwond. How could he play such a part for so long with all the darkness growing inside him? "That's not what it told you. Look at me! It wouldn't let me near it!" His voice boomed and blew some of the crystals on the floor toward the wall.

"I'm your flesh and blood. Your daughter. Did you really ever care for me or was I a pawn; a means to build your power?"

Her feet lifted off the ground and she rose high in the cavern. Hank and Warlita forced against the walls of the cave. "I looked for you, searched Lols. I should have taken what was mine when you were a tiny baby not a mouthy teen."

She felt Hank inside her as he fought the force holding him against the wall, their connection growing each moment. She felt his thoughts and emotions. More and more shadows swirled inside the cavern. It wasn't yet time to use their connection.

"A route to power. That's all I am. My mother saved me from you. The wraiths can't take what is mine. Their darkness can only swallow what is left of life, plunge everything into darkness and death."

The cavern disappeared in the blackness as the wraiths swirled in Cyrus' hate, their forms so huge they blocked out any light. The murky, unharvested souls couldn't hide their desires from Terra. She harnessed their weakness and used the cave walls to display a wasteland. The shadows moved into Cyrus. Lighting cracking across the sky and lava creeping over the ground. "Is this what you want?!" she screamed, showing him what was in his soul, what the realms would become if he had his way.

"You are weak, a silly girl. I can create visions too." The lightning and darkness left, replaced by her world.

She dangled above it. The tree, the field, and poppies. She pushed into his head to see what had happened that made him who he was, but it was a dark fortress. She wouldn't get anywhere with the wraiths inhabiting him. "I didn't create that. I showed you the fuel that inhabits the wraiths. They fool you!" *Enough!*

Her world vanished and they were back in the cave. Gathering energy from

Hank, she pushed against Cyrus and fell to the ground, Hank and Warlita dropping behind her. The crystals on the floor flickered with a soft light. As Sulien, he'd said daylight would return when the crystals glowed. Was that what was happening?

Hank's energy pushed through her, mimicking her thoughts. *Light.*

"You want an epic battle between father and daughter. The energy of the realm walkers inside me. All powerful Cyrus. I don't want it. I never wanted it. Take it!"

His lips twisted into a malevolent smile. "There's only one way I can take your magic." A blade formed in his hands.

Terra held firm, the energy of the source strong inside her. Its hum steady and rhythmic. Her connection to Hank feeding her warmth and love. She lowered her head as if bowing to him. He thrust the blade towards her neck and stopped just shy of her carotid artery. "No, stand. You must fight!" Spit blasted from his lips, coating her face.

A chant entered her head from Hank's mind. It spilled from her lips. "Blood of my blood, light over dark. Blood of my blood, light over dark," she repeated. Hank's voice flowed from her head to the room, followed by Warlita's.

Light erupted from Terra in four distinct rays that enveloped the room. Energy left her, amplifying what was inside her. The wraiths screeched as they swirled towards the dark corners of the cave. The flickering crystals stayed static as light filled the cavern.

Warlita flashed to Terra's side. "Move the light away!" she screamed, her shield and sword gone, a metal canister in her hands.

Terra pushed the light away from Warlita, who escaped into the other cavern. Cyrus shielded his face and pushed against her. She was too strong for him, with Hank and the full force of the source behind them. The wraiths vanished, their unharvested forms elongating as they stretched one by one into the other cavern where Warlita escaped. The light grew brighter and shone from behind her where Hank stood.

Cyrus dropped to his knees as she rose to her feet. His body twisted and contorted as wraiths poured out of it, their shrieks sinking into oblivion until all had left Cyrus.

The light vanished and the crystals glowed the colorful, warm light of the source. Cyrus bent over on his knees. He lifted his head as Terra approached.

"I'm still a realm walker. You think destroying the wraiths would destroy me?"

"No," Terra shook her head, his attention focused on her. She and Hank connected, she knew his thoughts. There was only one way to reverse the spell. *Finish him.*

The Ring of Betrayal

"I'm sorry for what I have to do but I have to take what was stolen. Blood of my blood."

As the words spilled from her mouth, she portalled Hank behind Cyrus. A plasma blade erupting through his chest, Cyrus blinked, a tear forming in his eye as Hank stepped to the side. "You can't destroy me that easily." He pushed upwards, blood flowing from his chest, and stumbled.

His desire for power was his destruction, not her, not Hank, but she had to finish him. She and Hank worked as a team. Allowing his betrayal to fill her up and Hank's warm energy flowing through her, she opened her mouth and released a flame that coated him and curled behind him.

He hadn't expected her to be the one. Tears erupted from her eyes as flames devoured him. A wave of energy pushed into Terra, knocking her backwards to the floor. It wasn't soft and warm like her mother's. It was coarser, but not filled with hate.

She crawled to Cyrus' body as the flames subsided. Shock, love, empathy, and relief coursed through her as she leaned over Cyrus and buried her face into his hot chest, her body heaving as she wept. Cyrus was dead and, judging from his energy and the tear on his cheek, he understood in his final moment who he'd become. That's what she wanted to believe.

31

Kenya

Pegasus riders with daylight runes mounted and flew high into the air, spreading light downward as sunbeams that spread over the entire valley. It was so bright, Kenya squinted her eyes and glanced away, wishing she had a good pair of UV sunglasses.

Shrieks and shadows slithered into dark corners as light found them, moving them further and further to the darkest underground reaches of Marsidia. They didn't burn or turn to ash as she'd expected but moved further and further down and slithered through cracks in the ground, almost as if they were being pulled rather than escaping the light.

From her vantage point, darkness filled the valley. She leaned forward from her seated position against a tree trunk and watched the valley vanish into darkness and appear again as the wraiths found their way deep underground.

Light poked through cracks in the valley, spreading upwards until the realm was so bright even UV glasses wouldn't help her. Alex, who stood beside her, grabbed her arm and stumbled, nearly pulling her down. She glanced towards him and gulped hard as his body transformed in front of her. Wings ripped through his shirt as his legs and arms developed into muscular dragon limbs with claws. Light erupted from him. "Alex!" she called as heat spread over her body.

Alex's torso stayed human in appearance. The warmth from the rays surrounding him encapsulated her. She glanced to Mario and Dena as they too shone brilliant like the sun. She gulped hard as warlock eyes studied them. Alex rose into the air, his wings taking him high, light spreading downward. The warmth she'd felt from him stayed with her.

Light glowed all around her as she brought her hand in front of her face and swallowed hard. She glowed as bright as the others. Warmth and love filled her and a second heartbeat pumped inside her. Spots formed on the insides of her eyelids. When the spots vanished and the pulse stopped, she opened her eyes and puddled to the ground.

The bright light flashed its end and was replaced by the colors of the source, radiating upward. It was a constant flow. Unable to move, she couldn't explain what happened, except her connection to the realm walker parent she'd never met.

The Pegasus riders with their sunlight runes dismounted, followed by cheers. Alex descended from the sky. His wings and dragon limbs transformed back to human. With all her strength, she crawled toward him and brought an arm around his neck. Her own limbs felt heavy and it took most of her remaining strength. "They did it… We did it," she forced out between heavy breaths.

Alex, his words as breathy as hers, struggled to form the words, "What about Warlita… Terra… Hank…? Do you think… they're OK?"

She nodded, her head wobbled on her shoulders, feeling heavy as a bowling ball.

Warlita was her best friend. She had to be OK.

Terra

"His power is gone but he shouldn't be destroyed," Bane's words grabbed Terra's attention as she lifted her head from Cyrus' chest.

Never happier to see him. His body still bruised, his clothes ripped, and hair mussed, he'd looked better. He knelt near Cyrus, opening a vein in his wrist with his sharp teeth.

"What are you doing?" Terra asked. "You're weak and he's gone. Had to sacrifice him to —"

"It doesn't take much, but the window of time is short," he said, turning Cyrus' head and positioning his wrist above it. "Our blood heals. If used right away it can bring life back from the precipice of death. The window between dying and harvesting. For many years, I will see what he sees, feel what he feels, and hear what he hears." He glanced up at her, his expression solemn. "No one must ever know that."

She hadn't wanted to kill him, but she'd had no choice. It was the only way to take his power, which is exactly what he'd planned to do to her. If he'd ever found her, he'd have sacrificed her earlier. He as much as admitted that. She wasn't him and had remorse, so didn't stop Bane from doing what he felt he needed to. The caveat was that now Bane would know everything related to Cyrus. Vampire blood was tricky and had magical qualities of its own. Terra's lips curled into a smile.

His words were news to Terra. Yes, essence to a vampire was blood, but she had no idea one could bring someone back using vampire blood. Would that make Cyrus a vampire? "Will he be..."

Bane shook his head. "No. To be a vampire one must pass the precipice of death and make a choice to take a second life."

Ohh! She changed the direction of the conversation, almost scolding him. "How are you here in Marsidia?"

His lips curled into his devious smile. "I've tasted your blood, so followed you in."

This made Terra a bit uneasy. It was creepy that he essentially stole some of her blood. It wasn't really surprising though. "They let anyone in," she mumbled.

He chuckled.

Changing up the subject, she asked, "How are you alright?"

"Your friend. She shielded me from the light, gave me her blood to heal my wounds, and trapped the wraiths in a metal canister."

Terra glanced away from Bane and found Warlita standing behind him in the archway of the door. She jumped to her feet and wrapped her arms around her.

Warlita returned her affection and asked, "What do we do with them?"

"I... I don't know. Is there a way to destroy them, send them to the Otherworld?"

She turned her attention to Hank. They weren't done. The look on his face concurred with her thoughts. She had the connection to the source, equivalent to eight realm walkers, and the grimoire, and he had the source rune. It wasn't only about destroying the wraiths and 'taking back what was stolen' as the source said.

Strife and hatred were slowly killing the Serenity Tree, along with the barriers dividing populations. The veils and curtains a bandage for the troubles of the past. She unzipped the pocket in her backpack and pulled out the scroll, handing it to Hank.

He accepted the scroll and took her hand. "It's time." In the midst of everything she understood he didn't join her at the source when she first went as the source needed her not him. As he said, his job was to fight the beasts and give her safe passage.

On their feet she pulled him towards her. "Not yet." Pushing his braids over his shoulder with one hand, she brushed it against his cheek and over his lips. His velvety eyes met and melted into hers as he tilted his head and pressed his mouth to hers. His arms wrapped around her, pulling her tight as his hands wandered across her back.

"Eww! Don't you have something else to do?" Warlita snarked.

REALM WALKER

Terra and Hank parted, cheeks flushed. Terra smoothed her hand down his arm and took his hand. "It's time."

Together, they walked through the empty cavern, pausing as they reached the cavern containing the source. Colorful lights spread upwards like a neon sign. She glanced up at Hank and smiled. His firm, sharp jawline, accentuated by the braids that hung over his back, a couple falling over his chest.

He smiled back, squeezed her hand, and together they walked into the next cavern. The hum of the source filled the room and its jelly-like form poured around them, pulling them into it.

You made your decision. You don't need me to finish what you started. Images of her friends and the warlocks celebrating and cheering filled the sides of the Source's jelly interior.

Hank unrolled the scroll. His head voice flowed in the jelly surrounding them. *No, we don't. By the blood of the lycan's heart, eye of the harvester, wing of a dragon, horn of a fae, tail of a troll, tip of an elf's ear, fang of a vampire, and blood of Terra's father, we reverse the spell. We command all the veils and curtains dividing all realms dissolve and all magic return to the source from where it came.*

And so it is that all should occur as the pact of a blood sacrifice. The source rune shall stay and bind you. You are eclipsed souls that can't be separated by spells. I once said you can't give back what was given. The rune on Terra's chest will stay and she will, until death, be a realm walker. Together with your unique friends you will work towards peace and understanding. Each successive generation, she will bestow the realm walker legacy to someone pure and unfettered by greed and power.

Energy flowed out of Terra in the form of light as it meshed with the sentient blob and the grimoire dissolved in Hank's hands.

A drop of water hit Terra's head and rolled off. Water droplets hung in the air above the source and collected on the shriveled roots of the tree. In seconds they plumped, taking the full shape of the rune.

32

C aps flew high into the air, flung by the graduates of Provence Academy. Hyacinth's arm looped around Terra's neck as they squeezed each other in an excited hug. Finding their friends in the crowd, they banded together. Dropping her robe, Terra stuffed it in Rosette's hand.

Rosette pulled her in for an unexpected hug. Terra didn't fight it. They'd had their go arounds but Rosette had proven she wasn't so evil, or at least not as bad as Terra originally thought.

Rosette pulled Terra back, pressing her hands gently on her shoulders, the robes dangling over her arm. "I'm proud of you.

When I met you the first time, I wasn't sure you could do it but I kept telling myself if your father could destroy then you could rebuild and unite."

Those words made Terra realize what her father did was what really united the realms. They had a common enemy. Cyrus. After the cleansing, they put the tribunal together and started the seed of tolerance. It was pretty sketchy and rough around the edges. Hybrids still weren't tolerated, but they put children together who didn't see the differences and the adults learned to put their differences aside for the common good. From tragedy grew acceptance. "Really, I didn't do anything anyone else couldn't have done. I reversed the spells that created the divisions."

Rosette held Terra's face in her hands, an actual tear forming in her eye. "No, only you could have done that."

Not really. Someone else could have broken it if they'd found the original sacrifices used in the level 4 magic spells. That was something Gwond, or Cyrus, never sent her on a mission to find. Why would he? He knew she didn't need those things to rewind the spell. All she needed was his blood.

Cyrus gave her all the ammunition. He sent her on missions to find specific things by manipulating her. She giggled inside. She was more like him than she realized. She did the exact same thing to Halsey. Which made her think he wasn't so bad, even though he tried to kill her. Was he truly trying to kill her?

It was as if he wanted to get caught or wanted her to succeed. Maybe she had it wrong and he wasn't after the epic father/daughter battle, but wanted her to prevail. Somewhere inside him, she believed, was a part of him that wasn't so bad.

Bane gave him a second chance. He claimed Cyrus needed to pay for his crimes, death was too easy. Possibly one day she'd understand how lonely and hard his life was that caused him to leap over the deep end into a brimming cauldron of wraiths. "Do you think he was really that bad?"

"Life throws many challenges at us. Sometimes we make good choices and sometimes we make bad choices with good intentions and sometimes we just make bad decisions. I think for Cyrus it was a little of all those things," Rosette said, then pulled her in for another quick hug. "Go. Be with your friends."

Giving Rosette one last squeeze, she parted and rushed to catch up with her friends. She'd made a choice after she and Hank reversed the spell and didn't return to the others. She gave Hank the ascendant and her tiara. By her calculations, the moon should be in the right position in a day or two, and with Warlita's locater bracelets they could join the others. Together, they could all transport to Provence. She made a journey only she could, and portalled to the Otherworld where she left the metal canister of wraiths.

Terra caught up to her friends and they practically ran to Verboten with every other graduate. It was their day, and all realms were open. No longer did one need a passport to go from one realm to the next. Terra and her large group of friends settled against a circle of bench-sized gems. A starbomb in her hand, back resting against Hank.

"Cheers!" Halsey said as she took an open place next to Bjorn on the ground. She'd come a long ways since Terra met her. Never would she have considered sitting on grass. "To wherever our adult lives lead."

"Here, here," Terra said as each and everyone of her friends seconded Halsey's toast.

"What's next?" Meesha asked, holding a moonbrew.

Halsey took a sip of the cool blue drink Terra remembered was made of Verboten mushrooms and messed her up. "I go to college in Navarin and take the throne in four years. It will be a new Navarin!" She raised her glass again.

"Be careful with that drink," Hank warned. They were so in cue with each other, as his words mimicked her thoughts and likewise. That's how he knew she wanted to give all the magic back. That and she'd never kept it secret she had no desire to be all powerful. She wasn't a god but a commoner girl.

"I'll be staying here," Meesha said. "I'm taking Gwond's place." Her gaze settled on Terra.

Meesha would be great. It was bittersweet and it was the Gwond side of Cyrus that Terra liked. She didn't always trust him, but thought his intentions were in the right place. She never guessed he was leading her down a path to learn more and more about history and her place in it.

Hyacinth pushed her straight, dark hair over her shoulder. "That's great! I always thought you'd make a good instructor. I'm staying in Provence, too. I'll be living with Devan and working at the new blood store at Provence Square."

Caspen's head in her lap, he lifted up on his elbows. "I'll be in college in Aradia – political science. Like Halsey said, new and improved. We have a real chance to make a difference, but I'll be back every break to see Hyacinth." He laid his head down and pulled her face to his, meeting her part way.

Nalysse joined the group, sitting on the edge of a large red gemstone, with a fizzy green drink. It wasn't Aradian, Terra didn't think. Nalysse was moving out of her elf comfort zone. "I'll be heading to Sier to help manage a new Herbal Infusions, an elf remedy store. What do you think?" She flipped her hair and it hung to her chest in light waves. As an elf, she'd always had super long hair that had never been cut. She was definitely heading out of her protective elfin bubble.

Everyone stared at her, as if they had no idea how to answer her question, until Kinzo spoke. "It looks nice and fits you better." They'd officially broken up but a spark still existed between them.

Nalysse smiled. "It was Terra who made an elf with short hair stylish." She giggled. "Seriously, she made it OK to put old traditions behind us and progress into a new age."

Terra wasn't sure she deserved so much credit.

"What about you Terra? What are your plans?" Nalysse asked.

"I'm glad they let me graduate." She chuckled. "I'm going to college in Aradia, where I'll continue to care for Serenity Tree." It's where her mother was from and, as the loan realm walker, it seemed important to her that she continue her mother's work. Since the destruction of the veils and curtains, Serenity showed immediate changes. Its trunk stood more erect and its base wider, its branches stretched higher and longer, and its leaves were perky. Everything was connected. Terra's ulterior motive in Aradia was her interest in the darklands and Aradia's first inhabitants. It wasn't her need to integrate them into a society that shunned them, but learn.

Before she could head to Aradia she had to appear before the tribunal that now had five new members she'd handpicked from Lols, who had more than proved their worthiness in Marsidia, and five new warlock members. Which solved the even number problem the five from Lols created. Five representatives from each realm, the tribunal was now at forty-five.

Tomorrow was the day the tribunal decided what to do with Cyrus. Since they'd returned, he'd stayed in the custody of Drakonia. It was Bane who salvaged his life and Jukane insisted Cyrus stay there until the tribunal came together with the new representatives. He believed it would be fair and just if *all* realms were represented for Cyrus' sentencing.

Hank would be in Drakonia. Jukane offered him a sweet position as the first non-Drakonian ambassador. They wouldn't see each other as much but would always be tied to one another and she wasn't planning on giving up portalling. Drakonia was only a blip away. At this point in their lives and relationship, they wanted to take it slow. Their feelings for each other were complicated.

Inside, she wanted it to work, not only for now but long-term.

Kayln bubbled, "Me next! I'll be teaching Old Fae to first years at Provence Academy."

Dena, Warlita, Kenya, Alex, and Mario joined them, squishing in where they found room. "We are the first official tribunal members from Lols," Warlita announced, barely able to contain her excitement.

They'd earned it. No way could Terra have saved the realms and life without them, and that was before they told her about the light that overcame them. Warlita's job was different, she helped chant the spell that released the spirits of the realm walkers to inhabit the other four for a short time. She leaned forward and pressed her hand to the center of the circle, followed by everyone else as they hit hands in a collective.

Clyde and Cora ran into the center of the circle where all the excitement was. She'd given Clyde a choice. He chose her and Cora well, Terra felt she chose him. Now she had two ferrets who would be joining her in Aradia.

Kinzo swallowed a gulp of whatever he was drinking and raised his glass. "I secured a position with the newly formed EBSI." (Extrarealm Bureau of Security and Investigation).

Realm Walker

Terra couldn't be happier for everyone. Somehow, everything worked out. When she first moved to Provence, huge divisions and hate tore the realms apart. Hybrids and extra realm relations were taboo. Now those barriers were dissolved. There was a long way still to go, but progress had been made. The humanitarian battle was only just starting, but her hopes were that one day love and acceptance would prevail.

33

The Tribunal

As always, the tribunal was indecisive and argumentative, each representative coming up with a different solution. It was suggested Cyrus go back to Thraves and help Death, stay in Drakonia and help new second lifers adjust to being vampires, or even go to Verboten and mine the rivers for precious metals. They even suggested the vampires mind wipe him. No one suggested he go back to Marsidia, but none of their suggestions seemed fit.

Bane stood beside Cyrus. Never did she see him stand before the tribunal that voted him off because of his sketchy actions with Metford, the harvester related to Tania. She'd fallen through the weak veil and they hid it.

At the time, it seemed like a huge deal and it was, but Terra clearly saw now that nothing was that black and white. It was varying shades. Far more shaded and jaded than she could have comprehended all those months ago. Like Rosette said, some decisions are good, some bad, and some well-meaning. Sometimes they were also just selfish.

There were no cuffs on Cyrus as he had no magic, no connection to magic. It had been severed. It was just the three of them - her, Bane, and Cyrus - standing in the middle circle of Provence Hall. There was a tension in the room not usually present as most tribunal members remembered what he did. They were there for the cleansing.

Terra stepped forward and spoke: "Cyrus is my biological father. I don't trust him. I don't even like him. But he is my father and I want the chance to get to know him, not as my instructor playing a part, but for who he is. Even without magic he is still himself. I think the most fitting life for him would be to come with me to Aradia and care for Serenity Tree. It is the giver of life. What would be more suited to the person who tried to destroy life than to learn how to preserve it?" She stepped back.

The Ring of Betrayal

Judging by the shocked faces of the tribunal, no one expected that or new how to respond. Whispers erupted around the room between realm members. Finally, Alex stood. "I don't see why that isn't a perfect solution. He has no magic and magic is something I can see. There is nothing inside or surrounding him. He is a commoner."

Erin of the harvesters stood as Alex sat down. "He raises a good point. He is a commoner. We can send him to Lols."

That was the most horrible idea. People in Lols were only discovering magic and, without it, couldn't even see the realms. He'd manipulate and use them. Bad idea.

Cyrus spoke then: "Might I have a word? If you are going to argue over my future then might I have input? Even in Lols, the defendant gets to speak. Are we not as progressive as a group of commoners?"

There he went again. Even without magic he'd manipulate the situation.

"I'm not good, I'm not repentant, but I am Terra's father and I was robbed of the opportunity to be in her life. She was hidden for seventeen years. What I became was born out of oppression and love. I wanted what realm walkers never had. I went overboard because I could…" he paused and the room stayed deathly silent.

He tucked his hands behind his back and stepped to the side, his eyes fixed on the representatives the whole time. "During the time I spent with Terra as Gwond, I grew fond of her despite her attitude and drama. I know I tried to kill her, but if she is willing to forgive me it seems others can too. Vampires are given a second life. I, too, have been given a second chance. I'd like to spend it getting to know my daughter. The source wasn't wrong for choosing her. She is the perfect realm walker and I am but a mere powerless servant. You can take away my memories of magic and magical tools but don't take away my memories of her or the pain, or I may once again become who I was. Her mother was right to hide her from me but, had she been in my life sooner, I might not have become who I was, driven mad by sadness and pain."

The scars on his face and arm from the source, still not completely healed, would be a permanent reminder of his life on the dark side. The burns she'd inflicted had completely healed. Terra addressed the tribunal again: "I don't trust him and I'm sure he'll try and manipulate me as he is doing to all of you. Playing on your heart strings. You and our ancestors are as guilty as him, but I'd like to understand so we can all move forward. Understanding leads to acceptance and love. I don't expect he'll ever be brimming in love for me or anyone else. However, there's a part of him that did what he did because he wanted to be accepted as more than a slave to the realms."

Ohhs and ahhs erupted around the room, except from the Lols representatives. They nodded in understanding. Terra continued: "When I first came here, if any of you knew what I was I'd have been ostracized, maybe even cleansed, or at the very least sent back to Lols with Rosette. She had faith in me. We need to put faith in Cyrus. He's not a threat anymore." Sure, he still was because his words held power, but she could handle him because she was like him. Judging by the expressions of the tribunal members, she had successfully manipulated them, but it wasn't their faces that surprised her. It was Cyrus', who looked on her with pride. He was seeing how alike they were.

34

erra closed her arms around Noah and he lifted her off the ground with a massive bear hug. His hair wild pink, he'd developed over the last few months since she'd seen him last, especially his abs, chest, and back.

When he let her down she punched him in the abs. "What gives? You've hulked out."

"Your aunt didn't tell you?"

"No, wait. How does she know? It was her who OK'd you staying with us and no one's business that you're going to Aradia with me, but what should she have told me?" Terra gave him a skeptical glare and folded her arms across her chest.

The Ring of Betrayal

His eyes lit up. "I'm part dragon and part elf. Rosette is my aunt. My mother is her sister."

Noah had been her lifelong friend and much like a brother to her. Her father, a dragon, and his mother were friends who lived across the street. That's how Rosette found her. She'd stayed in touch with her sister over the years. She'd told Terra the story even though it wasn't exactly the truth at first.

Her sister, an elf, fell in love with a fire dragon. They escaped to Lols because extra realm relations and hybrid children were excommunicated and treated as if they'd committed a crime. Terra's mother grew up in Aradia with Rosette. She was to be the Aradian realm walker and born to be that. She fell for Cyrus, got pregnant, saw who he was, and escaped with the man Terra believed all her life to be her father. He was her father. That explained the close relationship between her father and Noah's mother.

"Where is your mother?" Terra asked, interrupting Noah as she hadn't heard a word after 'my mother is her sister'.

He gave her the look demonstrating he knew she was lost in her own world and hadn't even heard him. "My mother isn't ready or willing to come back to the middle realms, but she didn't want to hold me back from experiencing it. She said they are beautiful, but with too many bad memories for her."

Bad memories alright! It all came together in her head. When her father died, Noah's mom immediately took her in. Rosette always knew where Terra was and the strange social worker that forced her to move to Provence with Rosette was no social worker at all. They both knew the day would come when Terra would become the realm walker. Her hair stood on end at the revelation.

"Where's Rosette?" Noah asked.

Terra shrugged. "Tribunal stuff. We're essentially taking a prisoner with us to Aradia. He'll be under guard for the next twenty years." That was what the tribunal decided since his evil lasted twenty years. "He's also being fitted with a permanent comicay…" As the words left her mouth, she thought of something else.

The elevators. Had Cyrus created them? He as much as hinted at it when he confessed he'd searched Lols for her. With a permanently fitted comicay, he wasn't more than a thought away. Pushing into his brain she asked: *Do the elevators in Lols still exist?*

Is this how it's going to be? You barging into my head, erasing my thoughts. The mocking tone represented in his mind words.

She could be just as sarcastic. *Yes. I'm the realm walker.*

Silence persisted for a minute, then words filed into her head. *You mean the portals that take you anywhere you want in Lols? Yes, but not all.*

She inquired further. *Explain.*

I grew up in Thraves. I was their realm walker. The screen between the living and the dead isn't clearly defined. Sometimes the worlds mix. The portals, or elevators, were formed in areas where the energy of the dead builds like graveyards, mass gravesites, mass murder scenes. Things like that.

Terra pushed her hand over her mouth. Tania explained how she found the elevators at graveyards. She was sent to Lols to harvest lost souls. As a hybrid harvester, she harvested in her physical form. Pure blooded harvesters couldn't. His words were truth. They matched what Tania said and what Terra had seen for herself.

"What's going on with you?" Noah asked in concern.

"It's a lot at one time. But, hey, you're here and you're coming with me. I can't wait to show you Serenity Tree."

"It is a lot. I've taken in that I'm a dragon and an elf. The dragon part of me has wings, but as a hybrid I don't know if I'll ever fly. They are thick and strong, but short. I feel more like a flying tree lizard."

She was awful. So happy to see her friend, yet she hadn't considered everything he'd learned about himself in such a short time. "Hybrids are different, unique. So is being the only realm walker. We'll figure this out together... You remember the journal we found in my father's office?"

He nodded and gave her a what-does-that-have-to-do-with-anything stare.

She explained where her thoughts were at: "Marya and Matthia are Rosette and your mother's ancestors. That means you are a descendent of not only elves and dragons but the elvarin. Gwond was a good magic instructor and, even though he's no longer Gwond - his secret had been revealed and with no magic he's only Cyrus - he still has his knowledge. He can teach you how to harness magic and so can the elvarin of the darklands."

"Will they let him?"

She rolled her eyes. "Nobody lets him. He does as he does. Really, I'm a lot like him. Maybe if he'd had a better life and grown up with love, not the harsh reality of all the lies fed to him, he would have turned out different."

Noah smiled. "There're two of you. I think we all need help."

Two of them. She was the only existing realm walker and it was her responsibility to pass it on to someone worthy. As the only realm walker in existence, the world she created was still hers and she the only person who could enter. The grimoire dissolved in Hank's hands and when she returned to her world the book was gone. Pushing that aside, she laughed. "True power is in the words we speak and our actions."

"Speaking of that. Well, not really. Where is your hunk, Hank?"

"He'll be here soon." As the words left her mouth, there was a knock at the door. "We are eclipsed souls." She shrugged, blaming their connection for the sudden knock.

When she opened the door, Hank took her in his arms and their lips met. It was Noah clearing his throat that separated them.

Terra put her arms down and patted her sides nervously. Both her favorite men in the same room, meeting each other for the first time.

"Hank, Noah, Noah, Hank."

She read Noah's expression immediately. His eyes conveying: *Wow! I need one of him.*

Tomorrow was a new day. She and her two favorite men would travel to Aradia with Cyrus and his guard. Those were the details the tribunal was solving at the moment.

See you tomorrow… daughter, Cyrus said into Terra's head as she collected her two favorite men for a night of exploration. The realms awaited.

Heart of Darkness

Realm Walker Prequel Vol. 1

1

The lieutenant's scruffy beard lifted up, then dropped down as he spoke. He hadn't seen action in years, evidenced by the pouch hanging over the belt holding up his disproportionately slender bottom half.

I opened a portal in his office mostly because I could and partly because he hated it. Assigned with giving me tasks, Lieutenant Berker was a stern man who lived his life by the harvester book. I wasn't a harvester and, therefore, didn't follow their rules.

It irked him, making my exit in a teal flash of light dramatic and interesting. I'd be scolded later. My parents would hear of my antics first. Mom would shake her head in embarrassment and Dad would act concerned, as if taking their scolding seriously, then pat me on the back later. Mom, like me, was a realm walker. Dad was a harvester who sent souls choosing vampirism to Drakonia.

The Ring of Betrayal

The teal light vanished on the flowered walkway to an ordinary condominium structure in Rubina, Verboten, its modern metal frame and flat roof matching every other building on the street. I opened the glass door and rode the elevator to the fourth floor where I stepped off.

A vase of flowers sat on a stone table, accenting the light green shade of the walls and blonde wood flooring. I knocked on door number 412 and didn't wait long before a female troll answered the door, her round eyes puffy from tears and her pink tail plumage drooping. She sniffed to pack away the sadness and opened the door wide, inviting me in.

Harvesters send the souls of the dead to Tranquility if they were pure and the Otherworld if they aren't so pure or so good. They were also crime investigation techs. In other words, realms sent them evidence and they used equipment and tools to study and return their results to the realm. As the realm walker of the harvester realm, Thraves, my job was to mend realm problems before they spiraled out of control, investigate hands on, collect evidence if needed, and save souls not ready for death *from* death.

In this particular case, the child had fallen ill. The woman spoke as she walked me through the condo. "Last night," she swallowed, "he woke up with a higher-than-normal temperature and now," her voice quivered, "he can't move."

She stopped outside an open bedroom. The child lay on the bed. Another realm walker was in the room talking with the father, asking him questions and noting the child's symptoms. She was Marilisa the Aradian realm walker. Elves made healing potions.

She glanced at me with hazel eyes as I stood in the doorway, her long hair tied in a braid that hung over her shoulder, the color absorbing the green shades of the wall. All realm walkers shared those features. What made Marilisa unique was the point of her chin, soft lines of her jaw, square cheek bones, and pouty lips.

I saluted to her from the doorway and followed the mother into the child's room, one ear open to the symptoms: fever, rash, hard time breathing. I excused myself to search the house. It was my job to find out if the child was poisoned or if any other malicious act had occurred.

Nothing seeming out of place in the crowded room, there was no need for me. The sooner I finished this job the better. The family gave me the freedom to explore the house. It was always easier in these cases if the nosey residents weren't stalking around behind me.

The Ring of Betrayal

I pushed against a door and stepped into the bathroom, the counter and tub so clean they sparkled. Opening the medicine chest, several fae potions were along the top shelf and elf remedies stuffed on the bottom. A stool was tucked between the sink and bath. It didn't take a genius to figure it out.

I started with the fae potions. All full but one. A restorative potion. I guessed the mother used it to salvage her young looks for as many years as she could. Taking out the fingerprint light, I shone it on the bottle. Telltale small fingerprints were on the bottle and the lid. The other potions showed larger prints and fewer. It looked like the child struggled with determination to open the bottle.

Lifting the bottle, I checked the expiration date and rolled my eyes. It was two months expired. With a fae potion that was serious business. I brought the bottle to the bedroom where both parents and Marilisa poured over the child.

"Looks like this is the problem." I held the small bottle between thumb and pointer finger. I shone the light on it. "See those tiny fingerprints?" The parents gasped. I didn't wait for their excuses before I tossed the empty bottle at Marilisa who caught it in her hands. "He drank the whole thing."

Turning my attention to the parents: "I recommend keeping your potions locked and throwing out expired ones." I turned on my heel and left the family to wallow in their negligence. My job was done.

Light steps pattered after me. "Cyrus." The tone in her voice demanding, as if I had to answer to her, or anyone else.

I stepped into the hallway, not bothering to look at Marilisa. The door closed and her footfalls quickened. "What was that?"

Bossy! Bossy! "That was me doing my job."

"That was you being," she let out an aggravated breath, "you. Why are you such an ass?"

I stopped and hit the down button on the elevator and glanced into the eyes of the attractive realm walker. "Me an ass. Those parents are assholes. They are neglectful and careless. Better parenting, and a call like that wouldn't be necessary."

The elevator door opened and I stepped in, pushing the button for L1. "Coming?" I asked.

Her beautiful features marred with the scowl on her face.

2

I depressed the jelly-like comicay on my wrist and reported in to the lieutenant. The device worked for communication, among other things. It sent thought to thought messages. *The parents had an expired restorative potion the child drank. The Aradian realm walker has the bottle. The rest is up to her.*

Good job, he responded in an irritated brain voice. He meant the words, but hated how I didn't drop at his command or follow the realm rules.

Realm walkers were the most powerful inhabitants in any realm, yet we were relegated to frivolous missions and didn't even have our own realm. We didn't even get our own homes. Instead, we had to share a "family home" - meaning we lived with our parents until we found a mate.

I sliced the matter open and stepped into the inbetween. Any realm walker could do it, but they had little knowledge of how much power they had and never used it. I created my own world, fashioned it from the teal matter of the universe. It was here I came to escape. One wall was covered in shelves filled with various objects I'd found in the realms, all of them having a use and connection to magic. The opposite wall held books, some commoner, others family grimoires, scrolls of ancient times. There was so much more to the realms. History lost with time.

As a child, I played sick and spent my days exploring each realm. When I got older, I took the brave step to visit the Land of Lost Souls. The prison realm. Only it didn't seem much like a prison. It had green trees, valleys, highlands, large bodies of water extending from huge land masses. Our power was a beautiful thing.

Dropping into the red armchair, I studied the spine of the texts for the next one to read. I filled my mind with magic from all the realms. My aspirations were to take realm walkers into the future, show them all they could do, but I needed to be well-read and well-versed, able to defend my position.

My finger on the round metal object on the lamp table. I spun it beneath my finger before choosing a book whose writing on the spine was absent. The soft cover melted in my hands as I leaned back in the chair and opened it to the first page. It was a personal journal from a dragon queen: Myovi. The ink on the pages faint from the passing of hundreds of years.

Dragon queens held little power, as male dragons ruled the realm until after the

Great War. The secrets of her life were revealed as my eyes scoured each page. Her husband had taken another wife and she wallowed in her self-pity until she met a troll servant who showed her affection. Their dalliances unknown to the king. When she became pregnant, she sent a servant to Navarin for a fae potion that would abort the fetus.

The servant was caught and executed, but not before blurting everything out in fear of death. I squirmed at the method of execution. A sharp talon was ripped across the chest of the servant and they were disemboweled. Myovi was forced to watch. The last entry in her journal read; *My true love will not face death as I take my life to protect his.* I couldn't recall exactly where I found the journal as I'd searched so many caves in Sier, the dragon realm.

If I was a more compassionate person I'd have felt pity for Myovi and her fate, but it was a fate of her choosing. She always knew the repercussions, not only because she was cheating on the King, but because hybrids weren't welcome. Some existed and hid, most were banished to Lols, the prison realm.

In the current age, subspecies couldn't travel from realm to realm. They had a single passport on their chest that tied them to their birth and subspecies realm. It hadn't stopped hybrids from being born. The only ones who could travel from realm to realm were realm walkers. We were created for that purpose. A passport for each realm imprinted on our chests after we entered and exited a realm for the first time.

Stuffing the book onto the shelf, I grabbed the bag lying beside the table and unzipped the matter, leaving my inbetween world and entering Thraves. I wasn't happy with my lot in life but had acquaintances. Calling them friends would be an overstatement. Metford, a young harvester and fledgling instructor in the art of harvesting, was one of those acquaintances. His legs hung over the cliff as I strode toward him.

Chestnut hair flowed over his back, the sleeves of his plaid, button-up shirt rolled to his elbows. I sat next to him, my legs dangling over the cliff beside his. Chilly air swept over us and a dusting of snow covered the higher peaks of the realm. The drop wasn't far before the valley rose into more midland mountains. The range spread for miles, slanted trees with sparse leaves dotted the landscape. The sun setting, purple and pink spread across the sky, giving way to shades of red and gold. Birds flew over the mountains, settling in the valley for evening.

I unzipped my bag and pulled out a drink made from the hops of Canida. One of the best perks to being a realm walker was the ability to not only go to any realm but to go anywhere in any realm. Canida was the realm of the lycans, powerful and large wolves, and their alcoholic beverages were made for large people, meaning we only needed one a piece to feel the buzz. Two and we'd be stumbling home.

He took the drink from my hand. "I successfully walked my first fledgling through harvesting their first soul today," he said, unscrewing the lid. "A child. He died of a disease that caused festering blisters all over his little body." He took a large gulp, followed by a second, before he dropped the drink between his legs.

"Did he go to Tranquility?"

Metford's head swiveled and color swirled in his eyes as he met my gaze. "Of course. He was just a kid." The colors in harvesters' eyes made it possible for them to see spirits. They didn't harvest in their physical form, but in spirit form. Not only could their physical form not pass the veil between realms, but they were safer from evil entities doing it in their spirit form.

"I saved a child, too. His careless parents had an expired fae potion in their medicine cabinet. They were lucky it didn't explode or implode. Fae potions aren't stable past their expiration." I shook my head, both hands gripped around my drink.

He nodded. Our conversation got lighter as the Canidan drink loosened our speech. I lay back on the thin, mostly frozen, golden grass cover and watched the stars, the moon emitting its usual orchid shade. *We need to talk. Now!* My mother's bitter words filtered into my head. I sat up and swallowed the last of my drink. "I gotta go."

"It's about that time for me too," he responded, scooting his legs over the side of the cliff and getting to his feet.

"You want a portal home?"

His eyes shifted as if deep in thought. Usually he turned me down. "Actually, I will. Thanks, Cyrus."

With a wave of my hands a portal opened around his tall frame then swallowed him as it vanished. I opened another portal for myself that landed me in my living room with an angry mom, hands on her hips and a scowl on her face.